KIAMICHI REFUGE

Book One

of the

Kiamichi Survival Series

C.A. HENRY

Kiamichi Refuge: Book 1 of the Kiamichi Survival Series
Copyright 2016 by Carol A. Madding
All Rights Reserved

Cover art by Hristo Argirov Kovatliev

Graphics by Cassandra N. Bailey

Editing by Hope Springs Editing

ACKNOWLEDGEMENTS

So much goes into writing a book that few people could do it alone and still do it well. I know I certainly couldn't, so I wish to thank my four beta readers: Jack Madding for being a sounding board for a lot of crazy ideas, Laura Gibson for her eagle eye, Richard Dennis for his expertise in firearms, and Scott Kenney who was on board from the start and also provided technical assistance. What Scott doesn't already know about computers, he will figure out. I could not have managed without his help. All of them offered valuable suggestions, most of which I took, and encouraged me throughout the process.

In Loving Memory of

James Matthew

Our Friend,
Our Brother

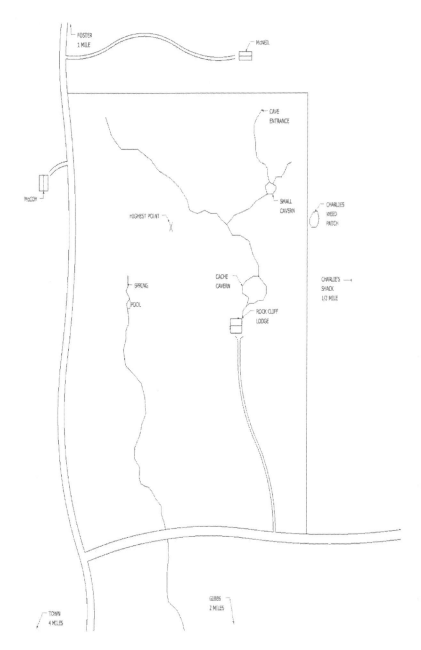

FOSTER
1 MILE

McNEIL

CAVE
ENTRANCE

McCOY

SMALL
CAVERN

CHARLIES
WEED
PATCH

HIGHEST POINT

SPRING

CACHE
CAVERN

CHARLIE'S →
SHACK
1/2 MILE

POOL

ROCK CLIFF
LODGE

TOWN
4 MILES

GIBBS
2 MILES

The Lodge Overview

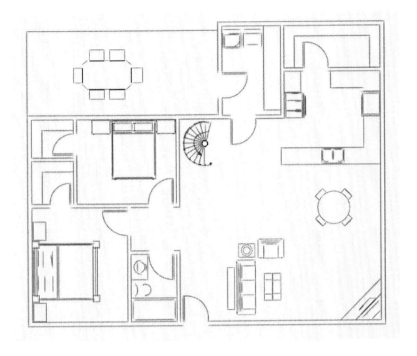

First Floor of the Lodge

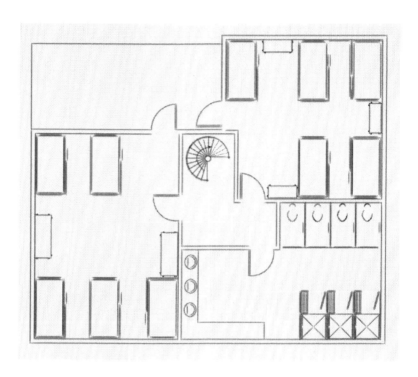

Second Floor of
the Lodge

The Town of Kanichi Springs
Population Before the Collapse: 472

Prologue
Early March

Wheeling her compact car into the driveway, Erin Miller jumped out and was running toward the door before she even thought to turn off the engine. Then kindly Mr. Hamlin stepped out onto the porch, and she realized from the look on his face that she was already too late.

"Erin, I'm so sorry. He's gone," the tall, lanky old gentleman whispered.

"What happened? I was here for his birthday only last month, and he seemed fine. I spoke with him just last week. He sounded tired, but not sick." Erin asked, bewildered. "He can't be gone. He just can't."

Leading Erin to the chairs on her uncle's front porch, Mr. Hamlin then went to Erin's car and turned it off. He returned, bringing her the keys, and sat down beside her.

"The cancer came back. He didn't want you to worry, so he kept it to himself. He spent the last few months finishing his book and getting ready to die. Somehow, he managed to fool most people right up until about two weeks ago. That's when the pain got really bad and his doctor insisted on in-home hospice care. There were two nurses with him at the end."

The elderly attorney ran his fingers through his thick white hair, then patted Erin's hand. "He was on morphine and slept almost all the time the last few days."

"I'll have to make arrangements for a memorial service," Erin muttered, as reality began to set in.

"As soon as the oncologist told him that the cancer had already spread, Ernie planned for all of that. Erin, he loved you so much that he took care of everything ahead of time. The only decision that you and the funeral director have to make is when the service will be. Flowers, casket, music, and all the rest are picked out

1

and paid for. After the service, you and I need to meet to discuss the estate. Ernie took care of that, too."

* * *

Mr. Hamlin stayed behind after the other mourners left Ernie Miller's home in the small town of Kanichi Springs, Oklahoma. Almost everyone in town, as well as several people from faraway places, had attended the service, and many had come by the house to visit with Erin afterwards. The ladies from the church provided light refreshments and stayed to serve tea and coffee. Erin was in such a stunned haze of grief that she could hardly function, and she knew she would not remember later who had come to the service, if not for the guestbook they had signed.

Erin had held up fairly well through the funeral, but just barely managed not to fall apart as people offered their condolences after the service ended. She looked beautiful even in her grief, wearing a sage green suit rather than black. Green was Ernie's favorite color, and she wore it to honor his life.

Erin invited Mr. Hamlin into the study, where Ernie had researched and written most of his books. The walls were lined with floor-to-ceiling shelves filled with hundreds of volumes. Ernie's big oak desk sat in the middle, facing the window, and Erin ran her hand across its surface as though touching it could give her a connection to her uncle.

They reminisced briefly about the many practical jokes that Ernie had played over the years, and talked about all the trips that he and Erin had taken together. They had toured Europe, Australia, and New Zealand, and spent Christmas in Hawaii a few times. Then Mr. Hamlin cleared his throat and asked, "Are you ready to discuss the estate?"

Erin nodded, smoothing the sleek French twist that held her long, auburn hair off her face. She knew that no matter how long she lived, she would never stop missing her uncle. He had been her only living relative for over twenty years, and he had meant the world to her.

"Your uncle left a considerable bequest to charity, specifically, the church here in town and several Christian children's homes. Everything else, including the royalties from his books, goes to you. He gave me a letter to give you," the lawyer added, as he handed Erin a white envelope.

Erin took the envelope, holding it with her slender fingers. She closed her eyes for a long moment, then opened the letter.

My sweet girl,

You are going to be angry with me, I believe, because I didn't tell you that I was sick again. I just couldn't stand to tell you that the cancer was back, and have it ruin our time together when you came down for my birthday. I wanted one last happy time with you before the worst came, and I wanted a great memory for you to hold onto whenever you think of me.

I hope that you know how much I have always loved you. You are more like a daughter to me than a niece. Even if we had had lots of other family, you would have still been my favorite. You made my life fuller and richer, and anything I did for you was done out of love.

There are many things that I want to leave to you, and one last request. Mr. Hamlin will tell you about the first. The request is that you finish the editing work on my last book and get it out there as soon as possible. Maybe it will help someone in the hard days that are coming.

Always know that you were the best part of my life. I'll be waiting for you. Take care, and God bless.

Uncle Ernie

Sadness filled Erin's throat as tears streamed down her cheeks. Mr. Hamlin finished cleaning his glasses and gestured toward the side table between the wingback chairs that sat in front of the large oak desk.

"There are some tissues, Erin, if you need them. I can tell you from experience that the pain of loss will lessen over time, but it never goes completely away. There will be times when it will just hit you out of the blue. A picture, a smell, a memory will suddenly be there, and the grief will almost overwhelm you. Give yourself time, but hold on to the good memories, and remember that Ernie was happy to do everything he did for you. He loved you very deeply, and all he talked about the last few months was how he wanted you to be happy. So *do* it, Erin. Be happy. Do what gives you joy. It's what he wanted for you, so honor his memory by living a great life.

"When you're ready, we'll go over the details of your uncle's will, and the trust, too."

Erin pulled a few tissues out of the box and wiped her eyes, then blew her nose. Taking a long, ragged breath, she struggled to regain some composure, glancing out the window as the wind caused the shrubs outside to dance.

"You know, I had a slight suspicion the last few times that we talked that he was keeping something from me. I've been down here several times in recent months. When did he know?"

"The doctors gave him the news almost a year ago," the attorney said gently. "He didn't want you worry or see him suffer. Erin, I am so sorry for your loss. He was a good man, the best, and I know how close you were."

"He raised me after my parents died," Erin murmured. "Dad loved flying that old plane of his at air shows, and Mom went with him sometimes. It's been over twenty years since the crash. Uncle Ernie never hesitated. He stepped in, giving up so much to take care of a young girl who was drowning in grief, and if he ever regretted taking me in, I never saw it. He even moved to Tulsa so I could stay in the same school, then when I went to college, he came back here. He always supported me in everything I did, from 4H to marching band. He took me camping, and encouraged my interest in gardening. I hope he knew how much I appreciated him."

4

"I'm sure he did. He was very proud of you. He bragged about you to anyone who would listen." Mr. Hamlin looked down at the papers he held. "He wanted the best for you, and he made certain that you will be secure financially."

Erin blinked back her tears. "Yes, you mentioned a trust. What trust?"

"Well, the laws being what they are, he came to me when he knew his time was limited, wanting to know how to provide for you without having so much of the estate taken up by taxes and the cost of probate and such. I advised him to put his property in trust, which does not have to go through probate court. In actuality, other than the sum of money to charity, almost everything he owned is already in your name. He made himself trustee for life, and now that he's gone, most of his estate comes to you, to do with as you please."

Erin looked at him questioningly. "He always tried to look ahead, to 'be a good steward,' as he put it. I'm not surprised that he wanted to avoid letting the government get its hands on anything, if there was a legal way around it. He paid his taxes, but resented all the sneaky ways that the government uses to get more, even after you die." She paused. "But I am surprised that he left it all to me. What about his lady-friend, Lillie? I would have expected him to leave something to her."

"We discussed that. He considered leaving her a bequest, but decided not to do so. Lillie is wealthy in her own right, and she told him that she didn't need it. She insisted that he should take care of you and not worry about her. Besides that, she has already moved to Houston to be near her son, and Ernie told her not to come to the service, to just remember him the way he was before he got sick. The properties are of no use to her. Ernie really wanted you to have those, anyway,"

"Properties, *plural?*" Erin looked puzzled. "I thought he just had this house."

"Well, there is another more recent purchase, a cabin, actually more of a hunting lodge, which he purchased right before he learned that the cancer was terminal. It's not all that far from here, but it is, from what he told me, almost hidden in the forest, with the

5

closest neighbors a half mile away and out of sight. As long as he was able, he used it as a writing retreat. I am surprised that he didn't tell you about it."

"Not a word. It's odd, isn't it? He wasn't in the habit of keeping secrets from me, but now I learn that he kept two huge ones for the past several months."

"I suppose we'll never know why. He left all of his personal property to you, including both of the vehicles he owned, and as I mentioned before, all book royalties. He got out of the stock market, sold his bond holdings, and used the money to buy the lodge outright, so there's no mortgage. What was left is in the bank, but he hoped you would get it out to buy gold and silver. You are also the beneficiary of two rather substantial life insurance policies. Because of the success of his books, you are now a wealthy young woman."

Chapter 1
A Few Weeks Later

Erin reached into the back of Uncle Ernie's dark green Ford Expedition and retrieved the black case that held her laptop. The sun caught the red highlights in her long, wavy hair as she straightened, then arched her back, in an attempt to ease the tightness brought on by the long drive south.

Since the funeral, Erin had immersed herself in the final edit of her uncle's latest, and last, book. Being able to fulfil Ernie's deathbed request helped Erin deal with her grief. He had written nine novels and four nonfiction books, all dealing with human survival in catastrophic circumstances. The last book was almost ready to go to the publisher, and was a detailed guide to living through a societal collapse. Ernie had a doctorate in economics, and had done extensive research on the signs, causes, and effects of global economic disasters. He had often predicted that another, but much worse, Great Depression was coming, and only a small spark would be enough to set off repercussions that would be felt around the world for decades.

As she worked on the edit in her tiny apartment, Erin couldn't help thinking that editing could be done anywhere there is internet access. That meant that she could spend at least part of her time at the lodge in the Kiamichi Mountains of southeastern Oklahoma. She loved Tulsa, but she was a country girl at heart. The more she considered her options, the more she liked the idea of packing up and moving permanently.

She had been back to Kanichi Springs twice since Ernie's death, and each trip had further convinced her that she definitely needed to be out of the city. Her career as a freelance editor was going well, but the noise level at her apartment complex was a distraction she didn't need. The station for the police precinct was just across Riverside Drive, which made her feel safe, but the sounds from the nearby playground in the River Parks made it difficult to focus on her work. Add the noise from the traffic going to and from the casino or out 71st Street to all the shops and restaurants at Tulsa Hills, and it was a wonder that she ever got any work done. The decision to live in the lodge instead of the house in Kanichi Springs had been an easy one. The lodge offered the solitude and silence that Erin craved.

She had left Tulsa as early as she could get away that morning, held up only by having to turn in the keys to her apartment. Her friends had helped her pack the things that she wanted to keep. Everything she was taking fit into the Expedition. The rest, including her furniture, went to a resale shop owned by a friend's aunt. Another friend bought her little car.

The drive south had been enjoyable and the scenery was beautiful, especially once she got into the hills past Henryetta. She had enjoyed the higher speed limit on the turnpike, although the powerful engine in the Expedition made it hard to stay legal.

Uncle Ernie's lodge was surprisingly large. It was two-story, L-shaped, and had a deep porch in the front. Wide steps led up to the porch. Inside, there was an enormous great room with a rock fireplace. There were two spacious bedrooms and a bathroom downstairs, along with a combination laundry/mudroom, a large kitchen, and a walk-in pantry. The upper floor had a large bathroom that looked like it belonged in a college dormitory, which Erin decided was exactly what the whole upstairs resembled. Accessed by way of a spiral staircase, two huge rooms contained bunkbeds and chests, and Erin decided that the previous owner must have invited all his friends to come for the hunting and fishing for which the area was famous. The lodge was built of thick logs, and the floors were a lovely dark laminate that matched the logs, except in the kitchen, mudroom and bathrooms, which had ceramic tile the color of coffee with cream. Solidly built, it looked ageless nestled in a clearing on the side of one of the higher mountains in the range.

For the time being, she thought, *the bunkbeds can stay. I won't need the upstairs for the foreseeable future, and there are more pressing matters right now, like finishing Uncle Ernie's book. Oh, I miss him so much.*

Stopping in the middle of the clearing that served as the yard, Erin slowly turned, taking in the beauty that surrounded her. Forests of oak, pine, beech, and hickory covered the slopes of the Kiamichis; as far as she could see, green blanketed the sides of the mountains, with no sign of human presence visible anywhere, except a cell tower in the distance. She could hear birds singing, and noticed the slight sounds that the breeze made when it ruffled the new spring leaves on the trees.

These mountains are not big like the Rockies, but they are beautiful. Living out here will take some getting used to, but it's a welcome change. I know that this is what I am supposed to do, where I am supposed to be. She smiled, feeling contentment and gratitude seep into her heart.

As a kid, Erin had loved camping, and was looking forward to exploring the property. Her uncle had taught her to shoot at an early age, right along with how to clean her weapons and handle them safely. She decided that she would get into the habit of never going outside unarmed. There were bobcats, bears, and mountain lions in the region, and since the area was known for suspected ties to drug smuggling, she planned to carry a gun when she went into Kanichi Springs, too, just to be on the safe side.

After she unpacked her suitcases and put her clothes and shoes away in one of the downstairs bedrooms, Erin sat at the kitchen table and started a list of things to pick up in town. She hadn't done much cooking in Tulsa, since there were so many places to eat and always friends who wanted to get together. But here, she knew, driving into town to eat every day would be impractical, and she was actually a pretty good cook, so groceries were a priority.

The theme music from *Star Wars* made her jump. She grabbed her phone out of her pocket and grinning, answered. "Hi, Jen! I'm here, I'm safe, and I can't wait to show you the lodge!"

Jennifer Martin, an old high school pal, was coming down for a visit in a few days. The petite blonde sold cars at a large dealership in Tulsa, and had been Erin's closest friend for years, ever since they sat together at a pep rally in ninth grade.

"Great. I'm glad you had a good trip. Hey, Valerie is taking a day off on Friday, and there's no school, so she and Sarah are both coming, too. Do you have room for all of us? It'll be like the sleepovers we used to have."

"Sure, there's plenty of room. I can't wait!"

The two friends chatted for a while, making plans for Erin to meet them in town. "This place is hard to find if you've never been here before," Erin warned. "I'll have to guide you in. It's impossible to give good directions with so few landmarks, so I'll meet you, then you can follow me to the lodge. Just call me when you see the Kanichi Springs exit off the turnpike. You'll turn left at the stop sign, then stay on that road for about 25 miles. There's a grocery store on the highway, just as you come into town. We'll meet there in the parking lot."

"We're going to be in Sarah's SUV. From your description of the lodge, we'll need a vehicle that has a higher clearance than my car for the dirt roads out there." Jen chuckled. "When you decide to rough it, you go all out!"

***

Erin spent the next few days getting settled in. She swept the floors and dusted, then put fresh sheets on three of the bunks, making certain that her new home was ready for guests, and each evening, she worked on her uncle's book.

The four friends met at the grocery store, as planned, and drove out to the lodge. When they climbed out of their vehicle, the three newcomers stared open-mouthed at the view. They turned, looking around, astounded by the lodge and the green forest that surrounded them.

Sarah Logan, a tall, red-haired science teacher, was enthralled by the landscape, which looked like a lime-colored quilt draped over the mountains. "Oh, I wish I could bring my botany class here for a nature study," she sighed. "But we just found out that due to budget cuts, we can't do any more field trips at all this year."

"It's a pretty place, I guess, but what about snakes and mosquitos? The outdoors just has too many things that bite." Valerie

Davis dusted imaginary dirt off her designer jeans, and sniffed. "I can already tell that this is not good on my allergies."

Jennifer twirled around, arms outspread, and grinned. "I love this! It's such a relief to get away from the dealership and the pressure to sell more cars. Valerie, you can just keep your little bubble butt inside if you want. I'm going to enjoy all of this that I can. It's so beautiful, it almost hurts."

"And the lodge!" Sarah stepped back to take it all in. "It's way bigger than I imagined. It looks like it almost grew out of the mountain, nestled here on this flat ledge."

Grabbing their luggage, they followed Erin inside and upstairs. She gave them a quick tour of the house, then they sat around the kitchen table with sodas and some brownies that Erin had made, and planned their activities for the next few days.

"In the morning, I want to take you on a hike. There's a spring not far from here that feeds a stream, and there's a little pool where we can take a dip when you come back in the summer. It's still a little cool for that now," Erin explained. "I hope you all remembered to bring hiking boots. The terrain can be challenging in places."

"I saw a couple of shops that looked interesting as we came through town. Will we have time to visit Kanichi Springs? You know how I love to snoop around in antique shops and thrift stores," Sarah shrugged. "But if not this trip, we'll do another time."

"We can certainly do that. I already planned to show you around town. We don't have to punch a time clock, so we'll do whatever strikes our fancy," Erin assured her.

The next morning they ate a hearty breakfast of eggs, biscuits, and bacon, then packed sandwiches for their hike. All of them wore long sleeves, jeans, and boots. Sarah and Jen carried backpacks for the lunches.

Sarah sprayed herself all over, then offered her spray bottle to the others. "This is citronella essential oil mixed with water. It will help keep the bugs off. Shake it before you use it. Everyone should tuck her pant legs into her socks. It looks funny, but it'll keep ticks from crawling up your legs."

Erin checked her rifle and clipped a sling on it so she could have her hands free. Her Glock 21 was in a holster on her right side. Jennifer, the only other one who was armed, put her Springfield XD-M in her holster.

"It's probably too early for snakes to be out, but there are bobcats and mountain lions in the area. The bear population isn't big, but it's growing. With four of us, we'll make enough noise that they won't bother us," Erin explained. "I hope."

Valerie saw Jen's gun and asked, "Why do you have that, Jen?"

"I work in a business that requires me to go on test drives, alone with strangers. I also leave the lot after dark sometimes, and I refuse to be without my trusty 9mm. I have never needed to even show it to discourage trouble, much less use it, but as they say, I'd rather have it and not need it, than need it and not have it."

Valerie shrugged. "I guess if you live in fear, a gun might make you feel better. I prefer not to think about all the bad stuff that probably won't happen, anyway. Worrying like that is not helpful."

Jen grinned at her, one eyebrow raised. "Trust me on this," she replied as she patted her gun. "I'm not worried about a thing."

***

The four women hiked around to the spring, enjoying the gurgling sound it make as the water danced over the rocks in the streambed. The water in the pool was sparkling clear, but when Jen stuck her hand in, she discovered that it was still very cold.

They hiked north to the back of the acreage, where they found a clearing and sat down to eat their lunch. After they ate, they headed east, then turned south when they reached the stake that marked the property line. They watched squirrels playing tag in the trees and saw a bobcat, but the only sign of bears was some old scat that Sarah noticed and pointed out. A light breeze rustled through the leaves, and an eagle glided, wings outspread, seeming to float effortlessly through the air.

Returning to the lodge, they approached it from the opposite side, not the way they had left that morning. Sarah stopped suddenly, and stared quizzically at the back of the lodge where it butted right up against the mountain. "Why did they build this that way? There's plenty of room in the front to have built it out from that rock wall ten or even fifteen feet. It almost looks like they started it in the wrong spot and ran out of room in the back."

"I wondered about that myself, but who knows? The back of the lodge actually touches the rocks. It isn't like that on the other side, where the mountain curves away from the lodge. There's a patio on that end, with a deck above it, off the second floor. The part that touches the mountain is the pantry. My guess is that whoever build it didn't measure it correctly." Erin scratched her jaw, then led them all around to the patio. "I want to get a new table and some chairs out here so I can sit outside to work when the weather is pretty. That old table might last a little longer, but the chairs need to be replaced. The cushions are torn and moldy."

Entering through the mudroom, they hung their jackets on the hall tree, then went through to the living room and practically collapsed on the sofa and chairs.

"I wonder how far we walked today. My leg muscles hurt," Valerie moaned.

Sarah laughed. "If you didn't sit at a desk all day, crunching numbers, you wouldn't be so sore now."

"What's for dinner?" Jen's tummy growled as if on cue. "I'm getting hungry."

Erin snorted. "You're always hungry. I planned to make my world-famous rigatoni tonight, but I'm beat. The little deli in the grocery store has great pizza. How's that sound?"

Sarah raised her hand. "I volunteer to go get it, if someone will go with me. Pizza sounds wonderful."

"I'll go with you." Valerie stood up and poked Sarah playfully. "You might get lost without my unerring sense of direction."

"While you do that, we'll throw a salad together. Come on, Jen. You can cut up the tomatoes and mushrooms."

While the others were gone, Erin and Jen chatted about mutual acquaintances and made a big bowl of greens, tomatoes, mushrooms, radishes, carrot slices, red cabbage, boiled eggs, and croutons. Jen caught Erin up on the latest antics of the "Martin Menaces," Jen's younger brothers David and Price. They were only a year apart in age, and were infamous for their pranks. They were students at Northeastern State University in Tahlequah, and would be returning home for the summer in a few weeks.

Valerie and Sarah made it back with the pizzas, and the aroma made them all eager to dig in. They laughed and talked until after midnight, then went to bed exhausted, but happy.

The next two days flew by. Erin and her friends visited a few of the antique shops in the tiny town, drove around the area a bit to admire the scenery, and talked almost non-stop. Then on Sunday afternoon, Erin stood on the front porch, waving goodbye as her guests drove away, headed back to Tulsa.

So, what do I do now? Erin wondered. *I'm almost finished with Uncle Ernie's book and the lodge is clean. Wandering around in the forest alone might not be a good idea, with spring starting. I don't want to become dinner for a bear or a big cat.*

I know something I can do. I'll find out more about the local fauna and their habits. Not knowing could be dangerous.

Erin filled her days with research about the area. Everything she found led her to something else, so she wound up learning about how black bears were migrating into Oklahoma from Arkansas, increasing the bear population in the Kiamichis. She discovered that the Kiamichis were part of the Ouachita Range and were believed to be older than the Rockies. She read about the settlement of the Kiamichis by the Choctaw people, and also found out that the Choctaw nation had been the first of the Five Civilized Tribes to be forced onto a Trail of Tears, and that the tribe had provided code-talkers for the European Theater in World War II.

She measured the windows and ordered some colorful curtains for the lodge, then rearranged the furniture downstairs. She cleaned out a small flowerbed in front of the house. She also spent some time in town, getting to know a few of the locals, but she finally realized that she was experiencing a strange restlessness.

Something was nagging at her mind, some little hint of a memory that she just could not quite pin down, causing a feeling of disquiet.

Waking up early one morning, Erin decided to sweep the patio and clean up the old glass-topped table behind the house. The leaves that had fallen months ago were damp and smelled moldy as she swept them up with an old broom that she found in the mudroom.

When she stopped to survey her work, the puzzle of why the house abutted the mountain came back into her consciousness. She had forgotten about it, but suddenly, the question that had hidden deep in her mind came rushing back: why in the world would they build right up against the rock wall of the mountain?

Hurrying into the lodge, Erin examined the back wall of the mudroom. The washer and dryer were against that wall, and nothing appeared to be at all unusual about the room. Going through the kitchen, she opened the door to the walk-in pantry. Wooden shelving lined the walls.

"Well," Erin muttered to herself, "There's not much in here, other than what I just bought. It's funny. Uncle Ernie was supposed to be a prepper, but this pantry sure doesn't prove it. Let's see. There's a canner, a dehydrator, some Mason jars, a pressure cooker, a Crockpot. A few cans of veggies, a bag of macaroni." Erin made a mental inventory of the various items as she searched the room. Leaning down and reaching toward the rear of a low shelf on the back wall, she pulled out an old box of cereal, but something else caught her attention. Just under the shelf was a metal latch. Erin slid the handle to the left, and the whole shelving unit moved a few inches toward her.

"What have we here?" she mumbled as a cool draft of dusty air wafted through the opening. Erin pulled the shelf further out, and saw a tall, narrow tunnel. Glancing down at the wooden shelving, she realized that the unit had hidden casters that allowed the shelves to move easily. The left side was on hinges that were firmly bolted to a steel bar, which in turn was bolted to the rock of the tunnel. The right side of the shelves swung out like a door. Stepping through the opening, Erin could see two large latches on the back of the shelves, which, she supposed, would allow someone to hide in the tunnel by locking the opening from the inside. Lower down, she could see that the smaller latch could also be opened from the inside, so a person could not be locked in. *Clever,* she thought.

Erin peered into the depths of the tunnel. It grew darker further in, where the light from the pantry could not reach. *I'll need a flashlight for that.*

Studying the walls and floor of the tunnel, Erin noticed a difference between the lower section of the walls and the upper part, from about four feet up. The lower area seemed more natural, while the higher section showed marks from some type of tool. Supports reinforced the walls and the ceiling, which also looked manmade.

Then it hit her: what she had been thinking was a tunnel was actually a cave, one that had been enlarged to allow for easier access. Someone had wanted to be able to walk upright through this, so there must be a reason.

"I have a flashlight, but no spare batteries, and I'm talking to myself again. I guess further exploration will have to wait until I can go to town. There is no way am I going into that black hole without a good light *and* a backup light. Nope. Not going to happen. Being stuck in total darkness is not my idea of a fun time."

***

As the sun's rays shot golden yellow across the sky the next morning, Erin rinsed her breakfast dishes and dried her hands. She grabbed a light jacket and her keys, and went to town. She bought three new flashlights and several packages of rechargeable batteries at a small hardware store. At the grocery store, she found candles, and bought a dozen, along with a box of matches.

Chapter 2
Early April

Armed with her old flashlight, plus a new flashlight and spare batteries, Erin took a deep breath and stepped through the opening to the cave. *As Uncle Ernie used to say, one is none, two is one,* she thought. She almost took a candle and matches, too, but chided herself for being ridiculous.

The air in the tunnel smelled fresher, perhaps from having the entrance open the day before. The quiet in the tunnel was broken only by the faintly echoing sounds that Erin made as she switched on her light and edged forward.

Curving gradually to the right, the cave went back about fifty feet, before it widened suddenly and sloped downward. Erin pointed her light down the slope, and saw a faint reflection ahead. A few more steps, and she found herself in a large cavern.

It was difficult to judge the size accurately by flashlight, but the strong beam barely illuminated the far wall. Incredibly, the cavern was far from empty. Shelves, made from stout 4x4s and thick plywood, lined the left side and were loaded with large plastic tubs. Dozens of five-gallon buckets were stacked to the right. More buckets, plus small metal boxes and long, cylindrical containers filled the middle.

Erin's eyes grew large as she took in the enormity of what was undeniably her uncle's survival cache. *Well, one of them, anyway,* she mentally corrected.

As her beam skimmed around the room, she noticed a large white envelope taped prominently to a big red bucket. On the envelope, written in blue marker, were large block letters that spelled out "ERIN".

Ripping the envelope from the bucket, she opened it and pulled out papers covered in her beloved uncle's handwriting.

Dear Erin,

Well, you found it. I figured it might take you a few weeks, but you would eventually figure out that there was something odd about the pantry.

I always thought that you were humoring me whenever we talked about prepping, but I was always quite serious. That's the real reason I bought the lodge. I knew that if I was not around to help you, you would need supplies and a safe place to take refuge when the brown stuff hits the fan.

Notice that I said, "<u>when</u>", not "<u>if</u>." Few people live an entire lifetime without some type of disaster taking place, and I saw too many signs of serious trouble brewing to believe that the future would be smooth sailing.

I don't know if it will be war, or a pandemic, or an economic collapse. I guess it could be an alien invasion or a zombie outbreak, although those are unlikely. It could be a natural disaster or some type of social upheaval.

But if I had to bet on it, I would say that the problems that are coming will be manmade, courtesy of the government, either ours or someone else's. Probably some combination of stupid decisions by bureaucrats, but trouble is coming, and that's a fact.

Enclosed you will find a map of the cave, at least the part that I was able to explore. Even a rat is smart enough to have an alternate escape route, so yes, there is another entrance. You need to familiarize yourself with the way in and out, and learn as much as you can about the area, just in case. There is a portion of the cave, toward the west, which I didn't get a chance to explore. You should do that, and add the additional caves to the map. Hopefully, there is a third entrance somewhere.

There is also a list of all the hidey-holes where weapons are stashed in the lodge. If you ever need one, you will need it in a hurry, so learn where each one is. There are fake books, hollow lamp bases, and decorative shelves with hidden compartments in every room, all containing a gun or two. The headboards of the downstairs bedrooms have guns in them, too. All of the guns are loaded, because an unloaded gun is no better than a rock as a weapon.

I have not had the opportunity to meet all of the neighbors, but I do know the McCoy family and the Fosters. The McCoys live in a little house about ¾ of a mile northwest of the lodge. Mac is a trucker, and looks like a Hell's Angel, but he's a good man. His wife is Claire, and she is really sweet. They have a little red-haired girl, Kyra, who is the cutest kid around. Get to know them. They have skills that could be very useful. Help them if things get rough. They've been good to me since I got sick.

The Fosters are a family I know from church, solid people who will probably contact you soon, if they haven't already. The McNeils are old friends of mine, and they live close to the north end of the property. There is no one I trust more.

You can also rely on Kenneth Abbott, the preacher in town. He and his wife, Terri, can be depended on if you need advice or help.

Be careful who you talk to beyond those I mentioned. There are some fine people in town, and some really shady characters. I think that Richie Baxter, the pharmacist, and Shane Ramsey, who teaches martial arts, are okay, as is Lydia Clark, but I don't know them as well, so exercise caution. There is something about Deputy Kline that strikes me as being off. He's an arrogant jerk, and sneaky, if you ask me, but he's the law in this section of the county.

There are some parolees around town. They're bad dudes, for the most part. Stay as far away from them as possible. I guess you know that a lot of marijuana is being grown in these woods. Don't go wondering around in the forest by yourself.

The supplies in this cavern were prepared specifically for you. There are tubs of clothing, and sturdy boots and shoes, and plenty of food to last for quite a while, plus guns and ammo, first aid supplies, and things like soap and shampoo. There may be others who come here for safety, so I got a several tubs full of fabric, and some patterns for simple clothing in various sizes. I hope someone knows how to sew on a treadle machine.

I hired an out-of-state crew to enlarge the tunnels and put in supports so they won't cave in. There is only one person locally who knows about the pantry entrance, and he will reveal himself when he decides the time is right.

A few more things you need to know: the windows in the lodge are polycarbonate, and will withstand small arms fire. The doors have a solid steel core overlaid with wood veneer, and the door-frames are also steel. If someone shoots a rocket at the lodge, you're in trouble, but anything less, and you should be okay. The back of the shelf that serves as the door to the caves is thick, high-carbon steel.

There are dozens of big flowerpots and several bags of potting soil on the deck. There are seed packets in one of the big tubs, for every type of veggie imaginable, and also some seeds for fruit trees. You have always had a green thumb, so use it. You will have to grow your plants on the deck, because even if the ground was not so rocky, a garden in the yard would just feed the wildlife. Up on the deck, the deer, rabbits, and other critters won't be able to get to your plants, and they will also get more sun up there.

Keep the papers in this packet secure and hidden. Your safety depends on it. Learn as much as you can, and use your head. There are books that you can refer to for most things that you may need to know how to do. They are in one of the tubs. Don't wait until you need to know something. Start learning now.

There will be some money coming in from my books. I strongly advise you to use that money to buy gold and silver. When things go down, paper money will be worthless.

You have good instincts, so don't second-guess yourself. I have faith in you and in the Lord, Who will watch over you always.

Keep an eye and an ear on the news, and pay attention to what is going on. You are smart enough to know when to batten down the hatches. May God keep you, Erin.

All my love,

Uncle Ernie

Erin glanced at the other papers in the packet, noting an inventory list, a list of where guns were stashed in the lodge, and the map. The cave evidently continued on the far side of the cavern, and the map indicated another, smaller cavern further in. It also showed another cave that branched off from the northwest corner of the big cavern, going west for a short distance and ending with a question mark.

Interesting, Erin mused. *I really don't want to investigate this by myself. What if I get hurt or lost, and nobody can find me? But Uncle Ernie always said not to tell people about prepping secrets. No one can go with me to see the caves without going through the cavern and seeing all the supplies. I guess I may <u>have</u> to go it alone, but I don't like the idea at all.*

Chapter 3
Late April

Lydia Clark unlocked the door of her shop and turned on the neon "Open" sign, then pushed back a strand of dark brown hair that had come loose from her ponytail. Straightening some bottles of shampoo on an end cap, she glanced around the modest store with a sigh of satisfaction. This was what she had always dreamed of doing. The town had needed a new business, and she needed to stay busy. The retail trade was in her DNA, with both parents employed as grocery store managers in Paris, Texas.

After going through a nasty divorce, Lydia needed to get away from her ex-husband and his pregnant girlfriend, who was less than half his age. In her early forties, Lydia set out for the first time in her life to be truly independent. The divorce settlement gave her the cash to start over, and when she passed through the quaint town of Kanichi Springs, she knew she had found a home. She saw the "For Sale" sign in the window of the vacant building and after an inspector assured her that the place was old, but sound, she bought it. She also bought a charming little house just a few blocks away.

Filling her diffuser with distilled water, Lydia added a few drops of Peace and Calming essential oil blend. Along with a complete line of quality oils, the shop carried diffusers, high-end toiletries, and unique gift items, many of them created by artisans in the area. For being in such a small town, the shop was doing well, with a few people coming from McAlester and even Fort Smith to shop for unusual gifts. During the fall tourist season, when people came through town on the way to the famous Talimena Drive, the shop got really busy. Lydia was considering hiring someone, perhaps a high school girl, to help out part time so she could have some time off.

The little bell over the door jingled merrily as the day's first customer strolled in, scanning the displays. Lydia looked up to see a young, pretty stranger in jeans, with a coral camp shirt over a white tank top. She had a beautiful complexion and big brown eyes. Lydia smiled and started toward the front of the store.

"May I help you find something?"

"Yes, several things, in fact." Erin grinned and offered her hand. "Hi. I'm Erin Miller. I just moved here from Tulsa. Your shop is lovely."

"Thanks. I'm Lydia Clark. I've only been here for a couple of years, myself, but I love it. If you're anything like me, you will never want to move back to the city."

The two women chatted as Lydia helped Erin find almost everything on her list. There were only three things listed that Lydia did not keep in stock.

"I can order those items for you, if you'd like. They'll be here in a few days and I'll call you when they come in."

"That would be great. I could order them online, but I doubt that the FedEx guy could find my place. It's pretty secluded," Erin laughed.

"Wait. You said your name is Miller, and you live outside town. You're Ernie's niece, aren't you?"

"Guilty. Uncle Ernie left me the lodge when he passed. I'm loving it out there, so peaceful and relaxing," Erin replied.

"I knew him. Not well, but I liked him a lot. I had heard that he bought a little place out in the boonies. I'm sorry for your loss, for the town's loss. We all miss his kindness and dry sense of humor. He talked about you all the time."

"So I've been told. He was my only relative, and it's good to know that others thought well of him. He was my hero in every way." Erin blinked back tears, and tried to smile. "I would like to have you go ahead and order those items, and now that what I *need* has been taken care of, it's time to shop for what I *want*."

Erin left the store with two bags of sundries, a diffuser and some oils, a painting of the Kiamichi River by a local artist, and a ceramic tray shaped like a large elm leaf. She also bought a pair of rustic candleholders. Lydia helped her carry her purchases to the Expedition, and as she watched Erin drive away, felt that she had just made a new friend.

Erin drove slowly down the street, taking the time to notice each building as she passed. Several had boarded-up windows, but most of the businesses were open. The town appeared to be doing okay, if not truly well. Erin knew that some of the coal mines in the region had shut down, mostly due to government regulations.

Parking in front of the courthouse, Erin removed her Glock from its holster and put it under the bags that held her purchases from Lydia's. As she hurried up the sidewalk toward the door, she passed a small cluster of rough-looking men who were just standing around smoking. The election board office and the tax office were both on the second floor, so after she took care of the property taxes, she stopped in to register to vote.

On her way back out, one of the men she had seen earlier suddenly stepped in front of her, and with a smirk and a glance at his companions to make sure they were watching, touched her arm and said, "Hey, sugar. What's your hurry?"

Only mildly alarmed, Erin stepped back a bit. "I'm always in a hurry. I'm very busy."

The skinny fellow grinned, revealing that his few remaining teeth were yellowed and crooked. "Now, that's not very friendly at all. How about we go somewhere and get to know each other?"

"I don't think so. Excuse me," Erin said coldly, as she tried to step around the man.

He grabbed her arm. Cold chills crept through Erin's body as she tried to jerk free, which only made the man's companions laugh. The stench of his body odor mixed with stale cigarette smoke almost made her gag. She was about to panic, when a deep voice interrupted.

"There you are, honey. I'm sorry to be late. Are you ready to go?"

Erin turned, looking over her shoulder. *That voice belongs to a giant,* she thought, as she noted that the man must be at least 6'7", with a pair of very broad shoulders. Muscles rippled under a blue tee shirt. His black hair needed a trim, and his eyes were the color of dark chocolate, glittering dangerously with suppressed violence. The high cheekbones and sharp angles of his bronzed face could have been chiseled from stone. *And he's a fine looking giant, at that.*

"Uh, yes. Yes, I'm ready. Let's go."

The giant stared pointedly at the hand that still grasped Erin's arm. Erin's assailant released her and stumbled back, intimidated by the size of her rescuer. He looked viciously angry at being embarrassed in front of his buddies.

"If we hurry, we can beat the rush," the big man urged.

He and Erin moved past the group, and when they were well beyond them, the giant whispered, "Just keep going. We'll enter the café on the corner and they'll think we had a lunch date."

Holding the café's door open, the big man followed her inside, where Erin breathed a huge sigh of relief. "Thank you so much for helping me. I usually travel armed, but since I couldn't take my gun inside the courthouse, this was one of the few times I didn't have it with me. That jerk just refused to take no for an answer."

"He's a convicted sex offender. Been a problem around here for years, with a seven-year gap while he was in the state prison. He and his pals like to hang out near the courthouse, I guess to thumb their noses at the justice system. Every one of those guys has done time."

Erin swallowed hard. "Oh. My uncle mentioned that there were some unsavory characters in town. I guess that was them."

"He was smart to warn you."

A perky young waitress approached. "Would you prefer a table or a booth?"

"Booth," the man answered.

Erin glanced up at him with a question in her eyes. He shrugged, then grinned. "To be convincing, we need to stay in here for a while. We might as well eat. Come on, I'll buy your lunch."

Once they were seated and their drink orders had been taken, Erin extended her hand. "Hi. I'm Erin," she smiled.

"Tanner. I'm glad to finally meet you. I heard about you for years from Ernie. When I saw you leaving the courthouse, I recognized you immediately. Ernie always had a picture of you on

25

his desk. I'm sorry that I missed the service. I was out of state on business. Everyone who knew Ernie will miss him."

"Did everyone in town know my uncle? They must have, since all I have to do is say my name and people know who I am. It's kinda nice, I think."

"Ernie was well liked and deeply respected by the townspeople. He got along with just about everyone, except the scumbags like you just met. Are you living in his house? Are you planning on staying in Kanichi Springs?"

"No, I'm living out at the lodge, and yes, I'm staying. I like the town and the peacefulness of the woods. Have you lived here long?"

"All my life, except for when I left for college. I went to OU, but I always knew I would come back here."

The two chatted through lunch, then Tanner walked her back to her SUV, subtly glancing around in search of the thugs. She used the button on her key to unlock the door, and Tanner opened it for her, leaning down to whisper, "I guess they crawled back under their rock. You need to stay aware of your surroundings, Erin. Be safe. I hope to see you again soon."

Erin nodded, thanked him again, and drove away.

Chapter 4
Early May

Over the next few weeks, Erin made a conscious effort to pay attention to the news on TV and the Internet. She began to understand that there was much more going on than she had previously realized, and that most newscasts were not telling the whole story.

Tensions were high in several regions of the world and small acts of terrorism occurred so often that they had become commonplace. Scandals abounded in political circles and corruption had become routine at all levels of government.

On the economic front, the news was disturbing. There were food riots in parts of Europe and unemployment rates were high in most of the world. A few large banks failed in Europe, and one failed in the US. Congress seemed paralyzed, doing little to solve the problems of rising debt and declining revenue

Erin selected a few of the books from one of the tubs in the cave, and started to educate herself on survival in a changing world. One of the first books she read was about situational awareness and how to defend herself. She knew that she needed to take some classes on that to really learn it, and made a mental note to check into what was available.

She ordered a plunger-like device for washing clothes, then went to McAlester and purchased several long garden hoses and three galvanized tubs that would work for baths, plus four smaller round tubs. The idea she had was to lay the hoses out in the sun and let the water in them get hot, then use that water to bathe or wash clothes or dishes. The idea should work for most of the year. She was new to prepping, except for what she had read, and she wanted to use Uncle Ernie's money for something that he believed in. He seemed to have thought of everything that would keep her alive, but she wanted to thrive, whatever happened.

As soon as the weather warmed up sufficiently, Erin filled most of the pots on the deck with potting soil, then planted onions, carrots, herbs, tomatoes, cabbage, green beans, peas, zucchini, and yellow squash. She only planted one pot of each of the last two, because she had read that summer squash does not preserve well.

A sense of satisfaction made her smile when the first tiny seedlings appeared. *I need to find someone who raises rabbits and see if I can get some bunny poop for fertilizer, and before these are ready to harvest, I need to get acquainted with that canner.*

She purchased a large quantity of stout fencing sufficient to enclose the yard and build a pen for a few goats, with barbed wire on the top, which would hopefully keep bears out. Uncle Ernie had included two Henry milkers in the stash, and Erin was eager to try them out.

She had lunch a couple of times with Lydia Clark, and despite the difference in their ages, the two were quickly becoming good friends. On her trips to town, Erin was careful to watch for the troublemakers, but she saw no sign of them. She didn't run into Tanner, either, which disappointed her.

***

In early May, Jen invited Erin to come to Tulsa for a few days for a visit. The four friends met for dinner at a little Italian restaurant, and Erin was surprised to see that Valerie had lost weight and gotten her blonde hair cropped really short.

"Val, you look great. Is there a man behind this transformation?" Erin teased.

Valerie's face burned hot pink. "As a matter of fact, yes. We've been out a few times, and well, I'm definitely interested."

"That pixie cut makes your eyes look huge. It's a cute style for you," Sarah commented.

Enjoying the company and the meal, the friends caught up on each other's news and joked about Erin becoming a country hick. "I like it," she admitted. "The solitude, the quiet sounds of nature, the fresh air. When I need human contact, I go to town or visit the neighbors. I go to church and have gotten to know several people there. I have plenty to do, with my container garden and learning about the region. It's a good fit for me. Now, when are you coming down for a dip in that spring-fed pool?"

* * *

Jen was off work the next day, so she and Erin spent the morning shopping. For lunch, they got sandwiches and pastries from a shop near Utica Square, then drove to Woodward Park for an impromptu picnic.

"This is something I've missed, living in the country. Grabbing take-out from any one of several places, I mean."

"Are you really happy, living in the middle of nowhere? I kinda envy you sometimes, but then I think about all the things you gave up, and I wonder."

"Things I gave up, like traffic jams, noise, and crowds, you mean?" Erin chuckled. "Yes, it's a big change, but it's worth it. Besides, when the zombie apocalypse comes, you'll have somewhere to run to."

"I know you mostly edit books about various worst-case scenarios, but do you really think that something horrible could happen?" Jen looked skeptical.

"'Not 'could' happen. 'Will' happen. I have been reading and researching a lot lately, and I am convinced that Uncle Ernie was right. History is full of disasters, like wars, tsunamis, pandemics, earthquakes. Governments are overthrown and economies collapse fairly often, in the overall scheme of things. I don't believe in zombies, to tell the truth, but haven't you noticed the bad stuff that is going on? Terrorism, crime, unemployment, the stock market's volatility, illegal immigrants, and racial division? It seems like we're teetering on the edge of a cliff, and it might not take much to push us over the brink. Few people are prepared for even a small crisis. Uncle Ernie tried for years to convince me to be prepared, but it took his death to make me take it seriously"

Jen considered that for a few moments, "I hadn't thought much about it, I guess, until just recently. I hate to dwell on the negative, but just the hint of a little bad weather does cause panicky people to rush around buying bread and milk. A major event would empty store shelves in no time. And if trucks can't deliver more merchandise, things could get dicey pretty quick. So, what should we do?"

"If it gets bad, you grab Sarah and Valerie and get outta town. Make your way to the lodge. Don't tell anyone where you're going, either. You are the only one with family here in town, so if your folks and the Menaces will come, bring them, too.

"In the meantime, get ready," Buy lots of ammo for your gun. In fact, buy another gun, at least one. Get a good pack and load it with all you can carry. I'll email you a list of things that any bug-out bag should have. We'll try to get Sarah and Valerie to prepare bags, too, but Val will be hard to convince, especially if she gets serious about her new guy. You might try to find out all you can about him, and we'll consider telling her to bring him, but for now, let's keep it quiet around him."

Jen gathered up the food wrappers and stuffed them into her paper bag. "This is a lot to take in, all this disaster stuff, but it's something that I've been stewing about for a while. I think, from some of the things she has said, that Sarah is concerned about it, too. Valerie has her head in the sand too much to see what's coming, but I see what you're saying. Something is brewing that just feels ominous. Let's not wait for you to email me that bug-out bag list. Let's just go buy a bag and you can help me put something together."

"Good idea. In fact, I tend to forget that Ernie's book royalties are going into my bank account and just sitting there. Three BOBs, coming up, and I'm buying! We'll start at BassPro, and pick up a few things at several different stores, so maybe nobody will start asking questions."

***

That evening, they all met for Chinese take-out at Jen's condo. Kicking back in the cramped living room, the four discussed how each had spent her day.

"School's almost out, and I am *so* looking forward to summer. This will be the first summer in years that I don't have to spend running to conferences and workshops." Sarah grinned. "I guess those budget cuts have a silver lining, after all."

"Well, you deserve some time off," Valerie responded. "Things never seem to slow down at the office. You'd think they would, now that tax season is over, but we're in the middle of the audit from Points South of Heaven. That IRS agent is determined to find a reason to hammer our client. She just keeps after us, even though she has been over the whole return at least three times."

"Hey, you're the one who wanted to be a CPA. When do you take the test?" Jen asked.

"Last week of this month. I'm ready, I think." Valerie ran a hand through her cropped hair. "I know people who will be taking it for the third time, but I need to pass it in one try. I want my own office after years of working to make my boss rich."

"I'm sure you'll blow the top off that test." Erin assured her. "I'll be your first client when you hang that CPA sign up. With the inheritance, plus income from the books, my taxes aren't so simple anymore."

"And speaking of inheritance, Erin bought us all something today. I helped her shop and put things together. We are all now the proud owners of our very own BOBs." Jen dragged out two backpacks, placing one in front of Valerie and other beside Sarah.

"Who's Bob?" Valerie inquired.

"B, O, B. It stands for bug-out bag. Of course, if you are away from home and trying to get back, it could also be called a "get-home bag." Erin plopped down in the middle of the floor, and pulled Jen's bag over. "We filled these with items that will help you get to safety in an emergency, like riots, or a terrorist attack."

"Well, surely that wouldn't happen in Tulsa," Valerie protested.

"*Au contraire,* dearie," Jen corrected. "Tulsa has had riots. Just because something hasn't happened in a long time doesn't mean it will never happen again. And let's not forget that there are oil refineries and storage tanks in town, and hydroelectric dams near the city. Those could easily become targets for terrorists. Plus, there's a history of earthquakes around here dating back to the 1880s, and even more tremors recently. We have tornadoes and floods and blizzards, too."

Erin leaned forward and spoke quietly. "Val, you may never need this bag. I hope you don't, but it's my money to waste. All you have to do is put it in the back of your car, or whatever car you are riding in. If you ever need it, the things that are in that bag could save your life. Humor me, please. I'll feel better knowing you have it. And it isn't just for end-of-the-world scenarios. People get stranded by car trouble, weather events, and earthquakes, all the time."

"I think it's a good idea, and I appreciate your doing this for us." Sarah took a sip of her soda. "I've been reading one of your uncle's survival books and I'm beginning to understand better that life can and will change suddenly. I want to be ready."

"Oh, Sarah, I'm so glad you're on board. Jen and I were discussing the economy today, and I want you all to know that if for any reason, you need to 'git outta Dodge', you're welcome at my place."

Erin picked up the bag in front of her and dumped the contents on the carpet. "I'm going to go through this one with you. All three bags are the same, so you won't have to empty yours. There's a set of lightweight camo in each bag, to put on over your clothes in case you have to move through the countryside. Each of you should tuck a pair of jeans, a shirt, socks, and hiking boots into your vehicle, too. Professional clothes don't do so well if you have to set out on foot.

"There's a first aid kit for obvious reasons, and three days' worth of emergency rations. There's a big knife, some paracord, and three ways to start a fire, in case you need warmth. There's a flashlight, too."

Valerie's expression made it clear that she still wasn't convinced, but she remained silent about it. Sarah pointed at a small package with something shiny in it.

"What's that silver thing?"

"That, ladies, is an emergency blanket, something developed by the space program. It'll reflect your body heat, or you can use it to stay dry if it rains or there's a heavy dew. And this," she held up a similar, but slightly larger packet, "is a sleeping bag made from the same material. They're so light, it won't weigh you down to carry both."

Erin completed her explanation of the rest of the items, and answered Sarah's questions, but Valerie had nothing to say.

Chapter 5
Early May

Glancing up at the quarter moon perched above the oaks, Tanner settled back in his camp chair. Peace flowed through him as he breathed in the mingling scents of the forest and the smoke from the campfire.

His companion added a small log to the fire. An older man, he carried his age with dignity. Talako, whose name means 'Gray Eagle', grabbed a couple of bottles of beer out of a red cooler and handed one to his grandson.

"So, you had a good trip? Did the seminars you presented go over well?"

Tanner took a long drink of his beer. "Yes, and there were thirty in attendance. From the comments when it was over, the officers felt that they got something worthwhile from it. We did a demonstration, too. There's something very satisfying about helping law enforcement officers."

"You were gone for two weeks. How did the search go?"

"I found exactly what I was looking for in Florida, a female pup with fantastic bloodlines. She's a beautiful little girl, and has already learned several simple commands. I am just glad I don't have to go to Europe now. Something is telling me to stay close to home."

"Speaking of home, *Hashuk malli[1]*, when will you marry and give me great-grandsons? You need to find your *chunkash anli[2]* and settle down."

Tanner raised his face toward the stars. "Grandfather, I have already met her. She's the one my soul loves. You'll like her, I believe."

"Who is she? Who are her people?"

---

[1] Choctaw for flash of lightning
[2] true heart

Tanner smiled. "Her name is Erin Miller, niece of *Tali isht holissochi*[3]. She was the reason Ernie moved to Tulsa for several years. She lives out at his lodge now."

"Bring her to meet us. Your grandmother is an *ohoyo*[4]. She will want to see for herself if you have chosen well."

"Soon, Grandfather. My heart is already hers, but I must find the way to make her heart mine. These things take time."

***

Late the next afternoon, Erin arrived home from Tulsa, mentally tired and physically exhausted. It had rained almost the whole way to Kanichi Springs, causing the trip to take longer than usual. Tense from concentrating for so long, she was glad that the rain had finally stopped. She parked the Expedition in front of the lodge, got out, and breathed in the clean scent left behind by the recent rain. With her bag in hand, she started toward the door, but stopped abruptly. Several large shoeprints led around to the side of the house. She leaned down to examine them, noting that there were two different sets, both large, but with different tread patterns. Sliding her hand under her jacket, she drew her .45 and held it beside her leg as she straightened, her eyes quickly scanning the clearing. Nothing moved, and the birds sang in the forest, telling her that whoever had been there was gone.

***

Erin had lunch with Lydia the next day, and the subject of life in a small town and Erin's isolated location at the lodge came up. They talked a bit about the prowlers who had snooped around Erin's lodge.

"They couldn't have been gone more than a few minutes before I drove in, because the rain would have washed the prints away. It only stopped raining about ten or fifteen minutes before I got home."

---

[3] silver pen
[4] wise woman

"That's scary, Erin. Do you want to come stay with me for a while? You know you're welcome."

"Thanks, but I have my guns. Do you think I should have called the sheriff?"

"You could have, but it would have been a waste of time. The deputy assigned to our area is worthless. On the other hand, he would probably at least file a report so there's a record of it. You know, you can't stay awake all night. I hate the thought of your being out there all alone."

The discussion on the pros and cons of living so far out on a dirt road led Erin to make a request of Lydia.

"I need to order several items online, but when companies use FedEx or UPS to deliver, the drivers can't find me out there. It's really the only major drawback to rural life. If I ordered some things, would you let me have them delivered to your shop? I could come pick them up, like we did when you ordered stuff for me before. Would it be an imposition? Some of the deliveries may be pretty big."

"Of course, you can. The delivery services all come to my shop frequently, anyway. I'd be happy to help, and I'll just call you when you have a package."

"That would be great. I really appreciate it, Lydia. Thanks."

***

After lunch, Erin decided to stop by the church office to see if Kenneth and Terri Abbott were around. Terri sometimes helped out as a volunteer secretary when their four older children were in school. The youngest, Kristen, was only four, and often went with her mother to work at the church building, which was right next door to their home.

Terri saw Erin coming through the door, and with a big smile, the petite brunette hugged her. Terri's brown eyes sparkled when she led Erin into Ken's office. Ken stood and shook Erin's hand, his white teeth gleaming through a well-groomed beard.

"Well, Erin, what brings you to town this fine day?" Ken inquired in his smooth baritone voice.

"I need some advice. It's not a spiritual problem, though. I just got home from Tulsa yesterday, a while before dark, and found shoeprints in the mud around the house. At least two men evidently scoped the place out while I was away."

Ken ran a hand through his thinning dark blond hair. "You should report it to the sheriff's office. And be extra vigilant. Keep the doors and windows locked, too."

"This makes me a bit anxious about you being out there by yourself," Terri interjected. "Is there anyone who could come stay with you?"

"Not really. Not at this time, anyway. Maybe I need to get a dog. Do you know anyone who might have one for sale?"

Ken glanced at Terri, and grinned. "As a matter of fact, our friend Tanner raises and trains police dogs. He's quite good, too. Several county sheriffs and police departments come to him to train both dogs and handlers, and he sells personal protection dogs, too. I don't know if he has any available right now, but we can ask. And we can also pray for your safety."

***

Tanner did indeed have a suitable dog. The young male German shepherd was one that Tanner had picked out to keep when the pup was only a few weeks old. The biggest of the litter, this dog was special. He was not only intelligent, he was also eager to learn. Tanner started training him early, and at almost a year old, the pup was way ahead of several older dogs. Not yet fully grown, he was a large, formidable dog already, and Tanner had no intention of selling him.

But when Tanner found out that it was Erin who needed a dog, he told Ken that he had the perfect dog for her. He didn't mention that Erin was the only one he would even consider as a new owner of his favorite pup.

***

"His name is Blitz. It means 'lightning' and it suits him. He's both mentally and physically quick. You'll need to spend some time here learning how to handle him, because he has learned some very specific commands, both verbal and using hand signals. I'll also need to observe the two of you together to be sure he's bonding well with you, and that he's willing to take commands from you as his new alpha."

Erin laughed. "I edit books from home, so my time is flexible. When can we start?"

Chapter 6
Third Week of May

"Blitz, strike!" Erin commanded, watching with satisfaction and a sense of accomplishment as the shepherd lunged toward Ian McClure's heavily padded legs, taking him to the ground. Ian, who owned a furniture store in McAlester, wore a bite-suit for his role as agitator. He was a childhood friend of Tanner's and enjoyed helping occasionally.

Erin told Blitz to release and the dog immediately obeyed. "Good boy, good dog, Blitz!"

Tanner had Erin run Blitz through a series of commands using only hand signals. The pup had a laser-like focus on her and obeyed without hesitation. It was obvious that a close and loving connection was growing between Erin and her new protector.

Ian ran a hand through his wavy black hair and commented, "He's doing well. He's the smartest dog I've ever seen. He catches on quick, and so do you, Erin."

"Thanks for helping out today. It's nice of you to make yourself into a target for those sharp teeth," Erin joked.

"You're very welcome," Ian chuckled. "Sorry to hurry off, but I need to get out of this hot suit and get to the store. We have a truck with a load of recliners coming in today. Tanner, catch you later, buddy. Erin, it's been a pleasure."

As Ian climbed into his pickup, Tanner turned to Erin and teased, "You kinda like sending this big boy to take down and tear up old Ian, don't you?"

"I confess that it's exciting to watch a magnificent animal work, doing what he has been trained to do. He's sleek and strong. I'm glad he's on my side"

Nodding, Tanner agreed. "That's the main reason I do this. These dogs are destined to be heroes. Raising them from tiny, helpless pups and watching them become police dogs or personal protection dogs gives me a great sense of accomplishment".

"You have a wonderful facility here. I like the way you have it set up. What's in that building over there?" Erin pointed at a large, boxy building.

"Half of that building is my living quarters. The other half is the office and a grooming facility for the dogs." He cleared his throat. "Say, do you have plans for this afternoon?"

"Nothing important. Why?"

"I need to take Blitz's litter-mate, Karma, to the sheriff over in Fort Smith, and wondered if you'd like to go with me. I'll buy your lunch," Tanner offered.

"Sure, I'd like that. By the way, Karma is a great name for a police dog."

"Yes, it is. It's a Hindu concept, and to paraphrase what I read about it, karma refers to the forces generated by one's actions, which determine the nature of one's existence after reincarnation. Most people think it just means 'what goes around, comes around', but that's only partially right."

"Say, there is something that I need to do, if you don't mind making two extra stops today. I need to go to a couple of places in Fort Smith, since we're going to be there anyway. That is, if you don't mind."

"Where do you need to go in Fort Smith?" Tanner asked.

"I need to buy some junk silver, and maybe some gold. I have too much money in the bank, and I want hard money, just in case. Uncle Ernie advised me to put most of my money in precious metals, so that's what I want to do." She gave him a conspiratorial look. "He also told me that I could trust people with the last name McNeil."

Tanner waggled his eyebrows at her and smoothed an imaginary mustache, trying to look like the villain in a melodrama, and succeeded in making her laugh. Then he checked his watch and nodded. "Yeah, we have plenty of time to do that. But remember, keep the amount for each transaction below ten thousand dollars. If it's over that, they have to report it to the federal government. You don't want them looking into your business too closely."

"That's true, and that's why I have been going by the bank occasionally and getting out random amounts of cash. So, when do you think I can take Blitz home with me? We've been through eight or nine sessions."

"He's ready. You're *almost* ready. If the next session goes as well as this one did, you can take him. I want him out there as soon as possible, before any more prowlers come around. I don't like it that you're alone."

"You never have told me how much I owe you for him."

"We'll worry about that later. Spend some time together, see how it works out. Then we'll talk about it."

***

The afternoon was sunny and warm, and Tanner proved to be good company. Their conversation was lively, as they argued over who was the best band of the 90s and discussed politics, finding that they agreed on most issues, but not all. They dropped Karma off at the sheriff's office, to the obvious delight of her eager new handler. Erin took care of purchasing silver rounds and old silver coins. At both gold exchange stores, Erin handed Tanner a wad of money. Then she and Tanner went in and each made a sizable purchase, so Erin was able to buy silver with all the cash she had, and still stay under the transaction limit. The seafood buffet at Catfish Cove was excellent, just as Tanner promised. Erin could not remember having a better time.

On the drive back, Tanner had the radio on, turned down low so they could still talk. Erin was laughing at Tanner as he related some of his boyhood antics, when they heard the radio beep for a news alert. Tanner turned the volume up.

"We interrupt this program with breaking news from Afghanistan. Taliban forces have attacked US and British forces at Bagram Air Base, following the apparent poisoning of hundreds of airmen by Afghan food workers at the base.

"More reports are coming in as we speak. Kandahar International Airport is also under attack. The airport, which is under NATO control, is sixteen kilometers from Kandahar City. It is believed that a passenger plane landed, then exploded near the main terminal. Members of the Taliban have breached the perimeter fences and are engaged in a gun battle with NATO forces.

"Stay tuned to this station. We will update continuously as more information becomes available."

Silence filled the cab of the truck after Tanner punched the off button on the radio. Neither of them spoke for several minutes as the shock of the disaster permeated their minds. Tanner reached over and clasped Erin's slender hand in his.

"Oh, dear Lord, have mercy on us all," Erin whispered.

Chapter 7
Third Week of May

Turning into the long driveway that led to his kennel and training facility, Tanner turned to look at Erin. "I am going to follow you home. You'll take Blitz today. We can do another session later, but I'll feel better if I know that he's with you."

"Bagram and Kandahar are a long way from here, Tanner," Erin murmured.

"I realize that, but hearing that news just made me think about how fragile life is. I don't ever want anything bad to happen to you. I care about you. I care a lot," Tanner admitted. "I don't mean to rush you, but you should know that I want you in my life. My whole life."

***

Tanner followed Erin and Blitz to the lodge and checked around outside, but found no sign that anyone had been in the yard recently. Then they stepped inside, and Tanner had Blitz check every room for intruders. "Blitz can do a check without supervision. It would be a good idea for you to have him do that every time you come home, while you wait down here until he's finished."

"Thank you for everything. I had a good time today, until the news came on. I'm going to cook up some dinner. Will you stay and eat with me?"

"I'd love to. Do you mind if I turn on the news to see what else they've learned, or will it upset you?

Erin shrugged. "I'm not one to fall apart easily. I'd rather know what's going on than walk around with my head in the clouds, ignorant and unprepared. The remote is on the table beside the recliner."

Not all of the news they heard was bad, but the situation in Afghanistan was bleak. Over four hundred British and American military personnel had been killed, many by poison put in their food by Afghans who worked on the base, and hundreds more were injured in the fighting. The sheer numbers of wounded overwhelmed the base hospital, which had one of the most technologically advanced trauma centers in the world. The main attack on the base was mostly thwarted by C-RAMs, which protected the base from rocket attacks. The ten Counter-Rocket, Artillery and Mortar systems on the base are equipped with FLIR (Forward-Looking InfraRed) cameras that can detect incoming rockets. The Taliban's Chinese-made 107mm rockets were mostly ineffectual against the C-RAMs, but at least two did get through.

Most of the casualties at Kandahar were innocent civilians on the plane and in the terminal. Rescue teams were still trying to dig through the rubble, so the numbers of dead and injured would probably continue to climb.

In addition, Marines at Camp Leatherneck in Helmand Province stopped an attempt by a suicide bomber, while British troops at nearby Camp Bastion were successful in preventing the sabotage of several C-5 cargo planes.

***

Erin and Tanner ate their meal of salad, garlic bread, and Erin's special rigatoni in near silence, as they absorbed the terrible news. They cleared the table and loaded the dirty dishes in the dishwasher.

"That was delicious. Thank you for sharing with me." Tanner patted his flat stomach. "If I didn't know that I'm Choctaw and Scottish, I would swear that I must be Italian. I have never tried an Italian dish that I didn't like."

"Me, either. I'm pretty sure I was Italian in a former life," Erin chuckled.

Tanner gently pulled her into his arms and kissed her softly. She stretched up to put her arms around his neck, and as she did, he felt the butt of her gun. He eased back and lifted the side of the loose plaid shirt that she wore over a yellow tank top.

"You got a license to carry that?" he asked, one eyebrow raised.

Erin grinned. "Of course. Doesn't everyone? Uncle Ernie taught me to shoot and take care of my guns when I was a kid. I'm a good shot, too."

"*Guns*, as in plural? Good. Oh, I remember now; you mentioned that you couldn't carry inside the courthouse. I'm relieved to know that you weren't joking about having a gun. With Blitz and guns, I won't worry. Well, not as much, anyway." He kissed the tip of her nose. "I better go. Lock the door behind me. I'll call you in the morning. Goodnight, love."

Erin walked him to the door, locked it behind him, and turned to Blitz.

"'Love'?" she pondered.

Blitz merely wagged his tail.

Chapter 8
Third Week of May

Instead of calling the next morning, Tanner showed up right after breakfast. Erin was about to turn her computer on when she heard the knock at the front door. Blitz was already on alert even before she got to the living room. She checked to see who was on the porch before unlocking and opening the door.

"Good morning, milady," Tanner drawled. "I was in the neighborhood and thought I'd check in on you."

"'In the neighborhood'? Really? What were you doing, visiting the third tree on the left?" Erin's eyes sparkled with laughter.

"You caught me. I drove all the way over here just to see your smile. And also to ask if we could perhaps go on a hike or something."

"Hmmm. Maybe, but only if Blitz comes along to protect me from wolves," she teased. "Let me get my boots on."

***

Erin led Tanner around the west side of the mountain. They strolled through the forest, holding hands when the path was not so narrow that they had to walk single file.

Climbing up on a boulder near the top of the mountain, they gazed out at the green vista spread below.

"I am so grateful to Uncle Ernie for this place. I miss him a lot, every single day, but this place helps me feel close to him somehow. I didn't even know about the lodge. He never mentioned it," she murmured.

"Right after he bought it, he told me that it was for you. He used it for a while, and loved it up here. I guess he wanted it to be a surprise."

"Oh, it definitely was. Now I just have to decide what to do about the house in town. Do you think I should put it on the market? With the economy in a slump, it probably won't sell quickly."

"It wouldn't hurt to try. I have a friend who's an agent. We could ask him what he thinks."

"Okay. I hate to sell it, but I don't need two houses, and I don't think I'll ever want to live anywhere but the lodge. I could use it for a rental property, but I really don't want the hassles. I think I'd like to talk to your realtor friend."

"I'll give him a call when we get back to the lodge. Hey, do you see that? Over there," Tanner pointed. "There's an area that's a different shade of green, right down there. Let's go check it out."

Tanner jumped down off the boulder, then helped Erin down. "Call Blitz. He's your dog now, and you need to reinforce who's alpha."

"Blitz, here!" Erin called, and the big pup raced toward her, skidding to a stop and giving her a doggy grin. They made their way down the hill toward the patch that Tanner had seen, stopping in a stand of trees.

"Uh-oh. Is that on your land?" Tanner asked.

"No. It's very close, though. See that stake over there?" Turning, she pointed to another stake. "And that one? They mark the property's east boundary. Ernie had it surveyed before he bought it."

"Okay, that's good. Do you know what those plants are?"

Before Erin could answer, they heard someone muttering. A few seconds later, an older man appeared and began to examine the plants, still talking softly to himself.

"Yep, comin' along real nice there. Won't be long now."

"Charlie?" Tanner called. "You old codger, what are you doing way out here?"

The man turned, a guilty expression on his face. His long, graying hair was braided and tied with a strip of leather. He squinted up at Tanner and Erin, then grinned, stepping closer.

"Tanner McNeil! It's good to see ya," the old fellow replied, thrusting his hand out to shake Tanner's. "I guess I'm really caught, ain't I?

"Indeed you are, but only by us. Erin, this disreputable old coot is Charles Farley, a friend of my family's. Charlie, this is Erin Miller, Ernie's niece."

"What's a lovely lady like you doin' out in the woods with this here unsavory character?" Charlie tilted his head toward Tanner. "But then, I guess it's better than bein' seen in public with 'im."

Erin smiled. "You two remind me of Dad and Uncle Ernie, always going on at each other. It's nice to meet you, Mr. Farley."

"Call me Charlie. I'm glad to meet you, too. Ernie was a good man. I'm real sorry fer yer loss."

"Thank you." Erin looked him with mock sternness. "Now, would you please tell me what it is we 'caught' you doing?"

"Well...," Charlie hesitated. "I suppose that would be checkin' on ma lovely plants here." He gestured toward the tall, leafy vegetation.

Erin glanced at Tanner, confused, then it finally soaked in. "Marijuana? You're growing *marijuana* next to my property?"

"Well, only a little. Just enough for my personal use. I don't sell it, not ever." Charlie looked sheepish. "I do have permission to be on that land. I'm livin' in the old huntin' shack."

"But does the landowner know that you're growing weed?" Tanner interjected, eyebrows raised.

"Uh, no. He lives in Atlanta and ain't been 'round in years. You gonna turn me in? Deputy Kline would like nothin' better'n to arrest me. Never has liked me, and the feelin' is mutual."

"Erin, it's your call, but I've known this old hippie my whole life, and if he says he isn't selling it, I believe him."

Erin sighed. "Charlie, you don't smoke and drive, do you?"

"Oh, no way! I ain't even got a car. I only use it at home, at night, to help with the pain when ma joints gets to actin' up, so it has medicinal purposes. It helps me sleep, and it makes me feel purty good, too."

"I have never used drugs myself, but I guess we don't need to report this to the authorities. We'll just pretend we didn't see it. Deal?" Erin offered her hand.

"Deal!" Charlie grinned and shook Erin's hand.

Chapter 9
Third Week of May

Tanner and Erin got back to the lodge about noon, so Erin offered to make lunch. "I've got some leftover pot roast and some bread that I baked yesterday. I could put together some sandwiches."

"Sounds great. While you do that, I'll call the realtor and see about maybe listing your house in town."

***

Wiping his mouth with a napkin, Tanner leaned back in his chair. "Hmmm. Let me see," he teased. "She's beautiful, classy, smart, *and* she can cook. What a woman!"

"Thank you." Erin blushed to the roots of her hair, then cleared her throat. "Did your realtor friend think that the house might sell?"

"He said it's a tough market, so it's hard to tell, but it's a solidly built house in a nice location, so maybe it will. He advised putting it on the market just to see what happens. Now, what are you doing tomorrow? And the next day?"

Erin laughed. "Tanner! I have work to do. I just got a new book to edit, and *you* have a dog-training business to run. Could we just slow down a little, please?

"Sure. I'm sorry. I promised myself that I wouldn't rush you, but it's hard. I feel like I've known you forever. I'll back off. If I forget, just sic Blitz on me, okay? He cupped her cheek with his hand. "I'd really, really hate to scare you off," he whispered.

***

Erin turned on her computer later that evening, and did some serious shopping. She ordered twenty sleeping bags and twenty cots, from five different websites. *No use setting off any alarms anywhere,* she decided. *I guess I did learn a few things from editing Uncle Ernie's books. Spread it around, and don't draw attention to purchases that label you as a prepper.*

She found a few websites where she could shop for all sorts of homesteading and off-the-grid supplies and tools, and ordered a few items that she thought might be useful, if for some reason the solar panels on the roof stopped working, then decided it wouldn't hurt to have more buckets of wheat and other staples. Another grinder would be good, too, and several more buckets of coffee beans. *I need my coffee, and if others decide to join me here, as it looks like they will, we will need a lot! There's still room in the cavern for more freeze-dried foods, too. I might as well spend Uncle Ernie's money before it becomes worthless. Express shipping is probably worth the money, too, under the current circumstances.*

Grabbing a sandwich and a bottle of Mike's Hard Lemonade, she padded into the living room and sat cross-legged on the sofa.

"Let's see if there is anything on TV, shall we, Blitz?" The dog cocked his head to one side, then plopped down on the rug.

Flipping through the channels, Erin stopped suddenly on a news program. "Early this morning, Kandahar time, two as-yet unidentified pilots flew over a neighborhood in Kandahar City, firing rockets into several buildings. It is believed that this was in retaliation for the attacks yesterday on Kandahar Airport, Bagram Airbase, and Camps Leatherneck and Bastion.

"The neighborhood was rumored to be a Taliban stronghold; however, many of those killed or injured were elderly people, women, and children.

"The two pilots, both Americans, are in custody and will be transported to the US. Charges are expected to be filed tomorrow. This is Bill Simpson, from Kandahar."

***

Two days later, with Lydia's shop closed for the day, she and Erin met in town and decided to drive over to Krebs and have lunch at one of the famous restaurants there. Erin ordered lasagna and Lydia had a small steak.

"What do you think about the situation in Afghanistan?" Erin asked.

"It's a terrible thing. I guess our guys just got fed up," Lydia sighed. "I heard that both of those pilots lost friends in the terrorist attacks, and the government didn't seem to be doing much about it. I guess they just had all they could stand, but they should have waited and not taken it into their own hands. What they did makes them terrorists, too, really.

"I know a guy who just got back from Bagram a couple of weeks ago. He said that they have a lot of fast food places on the base, ones like you would see driving through any American city, and they hire Afghan civilians to work there. They have Afghan military personnel there, too. He said he never trusted any of them."

Erin took a sip of her water, and frowned. "This is getting ugly in a hurry. I'm praying that it blows over, but I don't think it will. There was a lot of speculation on the Internet this morning about what might happen next, and videos of several mullahs in Muslim countries, ranting against NATO forces being in Afghanistan. There were even a couple of video clips about imams here in the US who were preaching about the start of a new jihad. They were encouraging violence, especially against Americans. People are angry all over the Muslim world."

Chapter 10
Last Week of May

After Erin dropped Lydia off at her little house on the south side of Kanichi Springs, she stopped at the drugstore in town to pick up a refill of her thyroid supplement. She gave the clerk her name, and when the pharmacist heard it, he came over.

"You must be Ernie's niece. I'm Richie Baxter. I heard you were living here now. How are you liking it?"

The two chatted for a few minutes, and Richie told her that he had just downloaded Ernie's new book. "It's really great. I have read every one of his books, and I think he was exactly right. Tough times can happen, and it looks like it won't be long before we find out just how tough. Ernie got me to thinking about survival, and I have a plan. Maybe sometime we'll get a chance to discuss it."

Erin sensed that Richie was a nice enough man. He was probably about fifty, of average height, a little overweight and totally bald, but his amber eyes were friendly and gleamed with intelligence.

She nodded, and agreed that they should talk soon. "I edited all of his books, and there are parts I can quote from memory. He was a brilliant writer, and I agree, the zombies could be on their way as we speak. I am trying not to let worry ruin my life, but I see the signs, too."

Erin ran a couple of other errands, but could not get her mind off what Richie had said. She was curious about his plans, and the thought that he had access to a lot of medications that might be vital to survival kept coming into her mind.

***

Several days later, Erin came home from buying groceries, and again found signs that someone had been there in her absence. Tracks just like the ones she had seen before led across the drive and up the walk to the front door. Scratches around the keyhole indicated an attempt at breaking and entering. She knocked on the door, and heard Blitz bark.

"*Well,*" she thought, "*Blitz sounds normal, so I suppose they didn't get in. I guess I'd better call the sheriff after all.*"

She let Blitz out, sat down on the porch, and made the call. About twenty minutes later, a white SUV pulled in. The uniformed deputy took his time getting out. The gaps in his comb-over hairstyle showed a sheen of sweat until he put his hat on, and his very pale blue eyes blinked frequently as he approached Erin.

"Wait!" Erin warned. "The prints are right there in front of you. And see, whoever was snooping around tracked mud all the way up the walk."

Kline continued to trample the evidence. The fingers of his right hand were in constant motion, turning and caressing something that he held. "Well, now, little lady, I believe I know how to do my job. I'm Deputy Sheriff Barry Kline. What time did you leave today, and when did you get home?"

As his questions continued, Erin felt as though she was being interrogated. The deputy continued to ask questions about her activities, without seeming to care about the evidence he was mutilating by walking on the prints. He was arrogant and pushy, treating her like a suspect.

"There are fresh scratches around the lock, Deputy Kline. Someone tried to get into my house," she insisted. "Aren't you going to dust for prints?"

"That won't be necessary." The item in his hand hit the gravel, and he paused to pick it up. It was an old-style cigarette lighter with a scorpion etched on it. "Whoever was here is long gone now, so you just need to calm yourself. Be sure to lock your doors. You'll be just fine," he replied in his overly loud voice.

"'*Fine*'? This is the second time this has happened! The shoeprints today look just like the ones from before," Erin protested. "Have other homes in the area been broken into?"

"Now, just relax. I'll file a report. That's about all that can be done right now. You should have called us the first time. Why didn't you? Do you have something against those who protect and serve, like your uncle did? I'd say your *dog* can take care of you." He strolled back to his car. "You be sure to call if you have any other problems, little gal," he smirked as he hefted his oversized belly behind the wheel.

Watching him drive away, Erin wanted to stamp her foot in frustration. "Arrrgggghhhhh! Mr. Deputy Sheriff Barry Kline, you are an incompetent jerk! Talking to me like I'm a child. A stupid child, at that," she fumed as she paced.

Just then her phone rang. Digging it out of her pocket, she took a deep breath and answered.

"Are you at home? Go turn on the TV. Hurry," Jen urged. "Call me when you've seen it."

Erin looked at the phone. "She hung up. Huh. And here I am, talking to myself again. Sheesh."

Rushing into the house, she turned on the TV, searching for news and finding plenty.

"In an unusual show of solidarity among Muslim nations, the leaders of Syria, Iran, and Saudi Arabia have called an emergency meeting of OPEC member nations to discuss possible sanctions against the US for the attack on Kandahar.

"Meanwhile, the death toll continues to rise for both the Taliban attacks on US bases and the rocket attack on Kandahar City."

Erin pressed the mute button on the remote and called Jen back. Jen answered on the first ring, and didn't bother with a greeting.

"Is this it? Is this the crisis we've been expecting?" she blurted breathlessly.

"I don't know, but it could be. It depends on what OPEC decides to do. We need to be extra watchful. Don't plan any trips, stick close to home, and keep your vehicle gassed up, for sure."

Erin paused to think. "You call Sarah, and I'll call Valerie. We need to warn them to be ready in case things go downhill. Let's stay in close contact meanwhile, okay? Hey, when is school out?"

"Sarah finishes up next Friday. She'll be on vacation for a while, but Val has her CPA exam tomorrow. Do you think you should wait to call her?"

"Yeah, you've got a point. Waiting one day probably won't hurt, and maybe this will blow over," Erin conceded. "I'll call her after the test. Besides, we might know more by then. No use distracting her at this point."

***

With most of her editing work finished, Erin decided to swallow her fears and take time off to go exploring. *At least I can take Blitz along for company*, she thought. With her Glock on her hip and carrying two flashlights, she double-checked that the doors were locked, then went through the pantry to the cave. Crossing the cavern, she chose the cave that Ernie had already explored, where he had found another way out. The passage angled down slightly toward the northeast, then curved more toward the north.

They came around a bend and could hear the sound of water flowing over rocks. Soon, the cave opened up into another cavern, but one considerably smaller than what she had begun calling the "cache cavern" in her mind. The little cavern had a pool in it that was about eight feet across, and the water she heard was seeping out of cracks in the rock wall to her left, then falling a few feet into the pool. She could easily see the sand and rocks on the bottom. Blitz lapped up a quick drink, then they skirted the pool on a sandy ledge that surrounded the water on two sides.

Continuing through the cave, they finally reached an opening to the outside. She peeked out, but had no idea where she was, so she simply retraced her steps and went back to the lodge.

Chapter 11
Last Week of May

Two days later, Tanner dropped in just in time for breakfast. Erin couldn't help noticing how handsome he looked, dressed in black jeans and a black tee. She told him about the attempted break-in and Deputy Kline's arrogant attitude.

Tanner was vocal in his disapproval of the deputy. "He has been a problem for years. I don't understand how he has kept his job this long. He doesn't do anything except strut around trying to impress people. He's just a useless waste of space."

"My thoughts exactly." Erin shook her head. "For a cop, he sure seems fidgety. He kept playing with a cigarette lighter, like he couldn't keep his hands still. And he actually called me 'little lady' a couple of times. He made it quite obvious that he thinks I'm stupid. That makes me so mad I could scream. I hate being talked down to!"

Tanner pulled her into a hug. "He's the stupid one. *Really*. I was in school with him. He cheated on tests and bullied other kids to let him copy their homework. I don't know how he ever made it through his law enforcement training. Maybe he bribed somebody, or blackmailed them. And that lighter? He's had that for years, and it's always in his hand. Pretty dumb if you ask me. He needs his hand free in case he has to draw his weapon."

Pulling away, Erin looked up at Tanner. "I guess you've heard the latest news. I'd like your take on it."

Tanner shrugged. "Things could go either way, depending on what the OPEC nations decide to do. They may just demand that reparations be paid to the families of the Afghanis who were affected, or they could decide on something more drastic. If that's the case, the poop may hit the fan. Our economy can't withstand a serious blow right now."

"So," Erin speculated, "If they do something severe, what's the worst-case scenario?"

"War, probably, but I don't think they'll go there. They would pay a high price for that even if they won, and I doubt they would win. They could impose some restrictions on how much oil they will sell us, or raise the price sky high. That would punish us, but not hurt them so much. It would certainly stifle trade. Every nation we trade with would feel the effects, but our economy would really suffer. The price of American goods would go up both here and overseas, and people would stop buying them. We sell a tremendous amount of grain to other nations, and with the price of oil high, the farmers won't be able to afford the fuel to run their equipment. And if they somehow managed to buy fuel, they would have to charge a whole lot more for the grain. Millions of people around the world could go hungry. The US as we know her might never recover."

"Are you prepared for something like that? Is your family ready? What will you do if things get bad?"

Tanner smiled and smoothed Erin's hair back from her face. "We're prepared. Remember, my grandfather was a close friend of your uncle's. My grandmother is an *ohoyo*, a wise woman. She knows the old ways that our ancestors used. My grandfather teaches classes for young people, how to live off the land, tan hides, stay warm in winter, live without electricity. They passed those lessons to my father and he taught me. And I have enough stubborn Scot in me to never give up.

"My grandparents would like to meet you, Erin. Will you go with me soon for a visit?"

She looked searchingly into his dark eyes for a long moment, then nodded. "Yes. I'd like that."

***

The next morning, she headed into town. Lydia had called to say that there were several large boxes in the backroom with Erin's name on them. As she stepped out of the Expedition, she glanced across the street and spotted the skinny fellow who had grabbed her by the arm at the courthouse.

He finished his cigarette, and tossing it onto the sidewalk, noticed Erin. His smirk appeared at once, but his eyes sparked with anger. He gestured toward his eyes with two fingers, then pointed at Erin. *I'm watching you.*

Trying to act as though she hadn't seen him, Erin forced herself to walk around her vehicle, determined not to hurry, and went into Lydia's store.

"Erin, what's wrong? You're so pale!" Lydia rushed over and looked out the big window. "Oh, that creep is out there again. Did he say anything to you?"

"No. No, he just made sure I knew that he was around. It's not the first run-in I've had with him." Erin described the confrontation that they'd had in front of the courthouse, "I think he's mad because I got away."

"You be careful. He and his buddies have been suspects in most of the crimes around town, and lately there've been a few break-ins. That one, the jerk, has been hanging around here quite a lot the last several days. He makes me nervous."

"Then you be careful, too. I wonder…someone, really two someones, prowled around my lodge recently. Two different times, I've found muddy shoeprints. You think maybe it's that bunch?"

"It wouldn't surprise me one bit. They're trouble."

"Who is that boy over there? He came out of the mechanic's shop, but when he saw the jerk, he turned and went the other way."

Lydia looked where Erin was pointing. "That's Micah. He's a good kid who's had a rough life. His parents are druggies, and right now they're both in jail. He's been in foster care for quite a while, maybe two or three years. The mechanic's name is Gus Jenkins. He seems like an old grouch, but watch his eyes. The twinkle gives him away.

"He's taken Micah under his wing and is teaching him how things work. Gus is really good at working on cars, but he also knows how to do electrical and plumbing. He's kind of a substitute grandpa to Micah. That poor kid needs Gus almost as much as Gus needs him."

Lydia glanced at Erin. "Pull your SUV around back, and I'll help you load those boxes."

***

Pinning her curls back with barrettes, Erin gave her reflection a final glance. The image staring back at her had fair skin and large brown, eyes in a heart-shaped face. Full lips parted to show straight white teeth. She applied some peach-colored lipstick, then moved through the lodge to check that the windows and doors were securely locked. She had already fed Blitz and let him out for a potty break, so she was ready.

Tanner pulled in a few minutes later. When Erin answered the door, he gave her an appreciative once-over and grinned, "You look fantastic. Are you ready?"

"Yes. A bit nervous, but ready. You said casual. Is this okay?" She gestured toward her black jeans and turquoise tee. Turquoise earrings dangled from her ears.

"It's perfect. We're going to be grilling outside. Nothing fancy tonight, just us and my family."

Erin peered up at him. "Just how much 'family' are we talking about?"

"Well, there's my dad's parents, my two sisters and their husbands, and a whole herd of nieces and nephews. Don't let the numbers scare you. They're all down-to-earth folks and nobody bites. They all want to meet you and are excited about tonight."

"Do they get excited every time you bring a date to a cookout?"

"I've never brought a date before. You're the only one. I want them to know you, and I want you to understand that they'll welcome you. I just hope my ornery nephews don't scare you off."

"Tanner, what about your parents?"

Tanner took a deep breath. "My dad passed away seven years ago. Mom remarried and moved to Florida. We don't see her nearly often enough."

Tanner's grandparents' land bordered Erin's on the north, and was only about a mile away as the crow flies, but going around by road made it a little further. When they arrived, Tanner hurried around to open Erin's door and help her out of his truck. The front door of the house opened, and a woman who was obviously Tanner's grandmother stepped out to greet them. Her gray hair was in a thick braid down her back, and her dark eyes sparkled as she grasped Erin's hand in both of hers.

"Welcome, Erin. I'm Julia. We are so happy to have you visit our home. Tanner has told us that you are the niece of *Tali isht holissochi*. He was our friend and we share in your loss." Julia's soft, pleasant voice was full of sincerity.

"Thank you. What did you call him? *Tali* what?"

"*Tali isht holissochi,* his Choctaw name. It means 'silver pen'. His writings are well-known in the area, and he was an honorary citizen of the Choctaw nation. He was very generous in giving to programs that help Choctaw youth. Come in. We'll go through to the back yard and join the others."

Julia led them through the house, then introduced the rest of the family to Erin. "This is my husband, Talako, and our daughter Rose with her husband, Will, and their children, Gina and Isabelle, who are five, and Wyatt, who's almost two. And over here are Dana and John. Their boys are Zeke, who is ten, and Tucker, who is nine. They're around here somewhere, probably getting into mischief."

The evening proved to be enjoyable. The men argued and joked over who deserved to have the title "King of the Grill" and which baseball team had the best chance of making it to the World Series, while the women set out potato salad, baked beans, deviled eggs, and several kinds of desserts, and got acquainted with Erin. The children were a bit shy at first, but soon, Erin was holding Wyatt and answering a hundred questions from the twins.

The adults ate steaks and the children had hamburgers. Tanner's sisters were both older by a few years, and both of them were beautiful. Dana's sons were typical boys, active and ready for fun. Her husband, John, was a history professor at Eastern Oklahoma State College in Wilburton. He reached a whole new level of "tall, dark, and handsome" in spite of the scholarly glasses perched in his nose.

Rose's twins were identical, but wore different colors, so Erin was able to tell them apart. Except for looks, they were as different as they could be. Gina was a bit of a tomboy, wanting to follow her older cousins and join in their tree-climbing and rowdy games, while Isabelle was very feminine and enjoyed reading and coloring. Wyatt was a sweetie, and liked anyone who would hold him on a lap or read him a story. Will owned a tractor dealership. His rugged good looks were a fine contrast to Rose's petite femininity.

For the first time in her life, Erin could see the joy and love that a large family could share, and she felt a longing to be a part of it. With no siblings and no cousins, her life had been devoid of that type of companionship.

When the children began to wind down, Rose started a Disney video for them in the house, and the adult conversation on the patio turned to the recent events in Afghanistan.

"Why hasn't OPEC announced a decision yet? The oil ministers are still in Riyadh, and we know that they've met several times, yet we've heard nothing. What are they waiting for?" Tanner's grandfather demanded.

"They must be considering serious options if they've deliberated this long without reaching an agreement," John added. "The longer it takes, the more drastic the sanctions will be, is my guess."

"When the announcement is made, if the sanctions are severe, the effects will be immediate. Panic, maybe even rioting and looting, are possibilities. If they cut back on oil sales to us, the price will go up and that will trigger general inflation. Or they might keep selling the same amount, but raise the price," Tanner mused. "Either way, we are going to be paying more for gas."

***

It was late when Tanner and Erin got back to the lodge. The night was lit by a full moon. Tanner held Erin's hand as they sat in his truck to talk and gaze at the twinkling stars. Finally, Erin was no longer able to stifle her yawns.

"It's been a long day. I need to let Blitz out, then I think it's bedtime for me. Thank you for this evening. Your family is wonderful."

Tanner pulled her into his arms and kissed her, softly and deeply. "I'm glad you enjoyed it. I'll walk you to the door, and wait until Blitz is ready to go back in."

Chapter 12
Last Week of May

After church on Sunday, the congregation had a potluck luncheon in the fellowship hall, located in the old building's roomy basement. Erin sat with an older couple she had met, but did not know well. Lee and Naomi Gibbs were in their seventies. Lee was tall, but slightly stooped, and had only a fringe of white hair. Naomi was plump, with short, curly hair and deep blue eyes filled with joy. They introduced her to their son, Jimmy, who looked like Lee must have looked when he was younger. Jimmy looked to be in his early forties.

The Gibbs family lived only about a mile from the lodge, and Erin was glad to get a chance to know them better. Ken and Terri Abbott joined them when the crowd began to thin.

"Have a seat, preacher," Lee invited. "We were just about to solve all the world's problems."

"Well, that would sure be something to brag about if you did, especially with the mess in the Middle East. Terri's cousin is in the Air Force, stationed at Bagram, and he says that all the Afghan civilians who worked on the base were forced to leave, except those who were charged with poisoning our airmen. Those people are being detained while we argue with the Afghan government over jurisdiction. Any Afghan military personnel who leave the base have to be strip-searched when they return. Tensions are high, to say the least."

"I heard on the news that we're sending another carrier group to the Mediterranean. Trouble is brewing, for sure," Jimmy added. "My boy is draft age, so I sure hope it doesn't come to that. If he was in the military, his sister would join, too, just to prove to him that she could."

"Where are the twins?" They didn't come home yet?" Terri asked.

"No, they stayed in Stillwater for a summer mini-session, trying to get more courses out of the way at OSU. They'll be home next week, though. Those two are so competitive, I think they're in a race to graduate, and see who has the highest GPA, too. Heather keeps trying to set Hunter up with her friends, hoping a girlfriend will distract him enough that he'll make a B."

"Well, tell them hello for us. We'll be praying that there's no reason to activate the draft," Ken promised.

"Me, too." Jimmy grimaced. "This situation is so volatile, anything could happen. We all need to be praying a lot."

When Erin went upstairs with her empty casserole dish, Angie Foster hurried to open the door for her. "Erin," Angie spoke softly. "Nolan and I would like to visit with you about something real soon. When could we get together?"

Erin looked a bit surprised. "Just about any time. Did you want to meet somewhere?"

"How about your place, tomorrow afternoon, about 1:00?"

"Do you know how to get there?"

"Nolan does. He is one of a very few people who were invited out when Ernie bought the place. We'll see you tomorrow"

***

Erin pulled the chocolate chip cookies from the oven and set them to cool, then made a pot of coffee. She was getting out cups and small plates when she heard a knock on the front door.

"We hope you don't mind that we brought our kids, Erin. We try to include them when we can, so they know their way around and understand what's going on. This is Paul, our eldest. He's a senior at the high school and works at the grocery store."

Erin shook Paul's hand, noticing that the tall, thin young man with dark blonde hair had the bluest eyes she had ever seen. Then Angie introduced the other two: Quinn, a green-eyed high school sophomore with wavy brown hair, and Amaya, who was a freshman. Amaya had slightly darker skin, straight black hair, and brown eyes, and looked nothing like the rest of the family.

The girl smiled, and explained. "I'm different, I know. I was blessed to be adopted into this family. I have Japanese ancestry."

"You have a beautiful name. What does it mean?" Erin asked.

"It's from a Japanese word that means 'bright star'."

Erin got out soft drinks for the kids while Angie poured coffee for the adults, and everyone grabbed a cookie or two. Once they were all seated in the living room, Nolan cleared his throat and looked at Angie, who gave an almost imperceptible nod.

"Angie and I have been wanting to get with you for a few weeks, Erin. Ernie and I made plans for our family to join him if things got too dangerous at our place, or vice versa. We were supposed to be each other's fallback if an emergency bug-out became necessary, but then Ernie got sick. The McCoy family is part of the plan, too. Did he ever say anything to you about it?"

"Not really. He did tell me in a letter that you might be getting in touch with me, but he didn't say why. Of course, I knew he was a prepper, but for a long time, I didn't take it seriously. That's probably why he didn't tell me."

"He always wanted the best for you, so I assume he left a lot of food and gear, but that's not why we're here. We have our own preps, but we would like to discuss whether you want to continue the group plan that we worked out before Ernie passed away." Nolan paused, and took a deep breath. "We're convinced that whatever OPEC decides, rough times are coming. You can't defend this place alone, if it comes to that, and Claire McCoy can't defend theirs, if Mac is out of town when things go down. She's pregnant, and they have a little girl, so Mac is trying to get the trucking company to either give him short runs or put him in an office job.

"The plan is that any of us who feel seriously threatened will contact the others by radio, and make arrangements to head to whichever location seems safest, bringing as much in the way of supplies as possible. We all have skills that would be useful. Mac is a ham radio operator and can work on radio equipment and almost anything with an engine. Claire is a fantastic cook and she cans, too. Angie is an ER nurse and knows a lot about emergency medicine.

We have a hobby farm, so we have that skill set covered. Our kids all take kenpo classes, and Paul has his black belt. Quinn and Amaya both have brown belts. I was a Marine for twenty years, and we all hunt and fish. We all shoot, too. We've taught the kids all sorts of things, like gardening, and they've all been to a survivalist summer camp at least once. Paul has been three times."

The three teens were listening politely, and petting Blitz. Erin was amazed at their respectful manners.

"This is a lot to take in." she replied. "I've been thinking about who I would get to help if I needed it, and I guess this is the answer. I'll need to know where your house is. Is it close enough to get to if I have to go through the woods?"

"It is. We're so relieved that you want to be in our group. We'll need to get together with you and the McCoys to work out details and plan projects," Angie explained. "We won't keep you. Thank you for the cookies, and we'll be in touch soon."

***

The next morning, Erin took Blitz to Tanner's facility for a refresher training session. Ian was unavailable, so Tanner put on a bite-suit and Erin ran Blitz through the whole series of commands. The dog performed perfectly.

Tanner smiled and scratched Blitz's head. "I'm super proud of this mutt. He's the best, the smartest dog I've ever trained."

"Which brings up something you've been avoiding," Erin scolded. "I know, because I did some research, that a dog like this can cost tens of thousands of dollars. I have the money, with royalties coming in from Uncle Ernie's books. The new one is at the top of the bestseller lists. You need to tell me what I owe you, Tanner."

Tanner looked perturbed. "To be honest, I never planned to sell Blitz. I wanted to keep him, but for you, I wanted the best protection available. I can't put a price on him, not for you."

"You have to. If you sold him to some stranger, what would you charge? I can't accept him as a gift, not when you earn your living breeding and training dogs."

Tanner frowned slightly. "How about this? You keep him healthy, and when the new pup I bought on my trip is old enough, we'll let him breed her, and I'll keep the puppies to train and sell. They'll be worth a whole lot more than just one dog, even Blitz, because with the bloodlines they have, those two will make some wonderful pups."

Erin hesitated. "Here's a better plan. I'll pay you $20,000 for him, *and* let you use him as a stud. I can't keep him otherwise."

"I don't want your money, but I have learned already how stubborn you can be. Okay. I'll use the money to prep some more, which will help us both."

"It's a deal." Erin stuck her right hand out.

"Deal." Tanner used the handshake to pull her closer for a gentle kiss.

Chapter 13
First Day of June

Erin went to town the next morning to see Richie Baxter. She had thought about what he said the last time she was in his store, and wanted to know more about him and the plan he had for a collapse. The pharmacy was busy, but she did eventually get a chance to invite him to have lunch with her. They agreed that Erin would pick up some burgers from the diner and bring them back to the drugstore so they could talk privately in his office. Richie put a "Gone to Lunch" sign on the door, and locked it so they could visit in peace.

"Richie, I've been meaning to get by and talk with you a little about what you said when I was in here before. You said you have a plan?"

"Erin, I am going to trust you on this. Your uncle was a big influence on me, and I was hoping to have more time to get to know him and learn from him. He got me to thinking about surviving if the world changed drastically, and I've done a lot of thinking about things he said in his books. I also read a lot of other books, mostly fiction, about things like EMPs and pandemics, and I realized that a pharmacy becomes a major target for looters if things like that happen."

"So what will you do? You have narcotics and other drugs in the store, and your life would be in danger if addicts or people who need medicine get desperate."

"I have decided that when I get the first whiff of the brown stuff impacting the rotary air impeller, I have to move it all out of here, and take it somewhere safe. I've changed the way that I stock the drugs. They are all arranged like normal, but in shallow trays. Those trays are actually lids for some plastic boxes that I purchased, and all I have to do is slide the tray out, put the box on it upside down, and turn the whole thing over. That way, I can have everything boxed up, still pretty much organized, in a matter of minutes. Liquid medications are in a different type of container, so I won't have to turn them over, and I have a big cooler for the drugs that need to be refrigerated. It's in the back room, and we sell bagged ice, so I'll just grab some and dump it in the cooler. The problem is, I don't really have a safe place to go once I pack it all up. Almost everyone in town knows where I live, so I can't take the drugs to my house. It wouldn't be any more secure there than it is here in the store."

"And you're wondering if you can come out to my lodge," Erin guessed.

"Well, yes. I am not sure of the exact location, but who would suspect that I hid the drugs there? I guess it would also mean that I come with them, because the druggies here in town would never believe me if I told them the drugs were gone. I think they would torture me for the location, so I'm not safe anywhere in town."

"I'd like a little time to think on this, Richie. I would love to help you, but I am not the only person who will be affected by your coming out. And I really don't know you well, but I will say that I'm inclined to tell you to come on. I think you would be an asset. I am just trying to make certain that it's the right decision, because it will be hard to undo if it's not."

"I understand." Richie looked disheartened. "If you decide to let me come, or even if you don't, we should probably not be seen together in town after today. People might figure out that we're friendly and come pay a visit to your place, looking for me. I don't want to put you in danger, even if you say no."

"Richie, I think you just put several points on the scoreboard. That you would be concerned about me, even if you're not to invited to come out to the lodge, says a lot about your character. I'll get back to you right away. And to preserve security, we'll just talk on the phone from now on, but be careful what we say. If I have to come into the store for anything, we'll act like we are just customer and pharmacist, okay?"

"Okay. I hope you let me join you. I promise not to talk to anyone about your place, regardless of what you decide. And thanks for lunch."

***

Tanner didn't answer his phone, so Erin took a chance and drove out to the training facility. He was working the new female shepherd that he had bought on his recent trip. She was a beautiful puppy, and showed real promise as a protection dog. Erin watched as he finished up the session with her, then strolled over to where she sat watching.

"What brings you out here today, gorgeous?"

"I need to run something by you, and it wasn't something we should talk about on the phone. I tried to call to tell you I was coming, but I guess you were busy. What did you name the new girl?"

"Moxie. She is as courageous as any dog I've seen, and doesn't back down." Tanner shrugged. "I have named so many dogs over the years that I'm about out of original ideas."

"I like it. Can you take a break, or should I come back later?"

"I'm actually through for the day. What's on your mind?"

"How well do you know Richie Baxter?"

"I've known him for about twelve years. He's a good guy. Why do you ask?"

"Apparently, he's worried about the possibility of trouble. He said he knows that if things get bad, he and his store will be targets for druggies, and he wants to come out to the lodge and bring the drugs from the store with him. I just don't know him well enough to answer, without talking to someone who does know him. Uncle Ernie said he thought he was okay. What do you think I should do?"

"I think you should tell him yes. His chances of survival alone are not good, and it isn't just druggies that he'll need to fear. Anyone who needs medication on a regular basis, like diabetics and people with heart trouble, will be frantic. If he runs out of something, and someone needs it, they probably won't believe him when he says he doesn't have it. Parents of children who need medicine will be also be desperate, and that's understandable, but it puts Richie in a bad place. He's always been honest with my family, and I have never heard anyone say anything negative about him."

"Okay. That's what I needed to know. Thanks."

"So, what's on your schedule for the afternoon? Would you like to take a drive and grab dinner somewhere?"

"Persistent, aren't you? Yes, I'd love to, but first, I need to call Richie and tell him that he just joined our group."

Chapter 14
Second Week of June

Erin threw back the covers and stretched. Sunlight streamed in the bedroom window, promising a beautiful day. *Life sure has taken some unexpected turns lately,* she thought. *A new home, new friends, a new dog, and Tanner. I miss Uncle Ernie, but I am going to do my best to do what he wanted me to do: be happy. No matter what happens, I'll try to find good in it.*

She had met with the Fosters and the McCoys a few times, and they all knew the evacuation plan, if necessary. All of the things she had ordered online came in, and although it had taken several trips into town, the items were safely stored in the cavern.

She had Tanner's family over for dinner and it went very well. The pots on the upper deck were full of healthy, growing vegetables that she could begin harvesting and preserving soon. There had been no more evidence of prowlers around the lodge, but she knew where Ernie had guns stashed, just in case.

She slipped on her house shoes, let Blitz out, then shuffled sleepily to the kitchen. Two fried eggs, toast, and two cups of coffee later, she was ready to start the day.

The Expedition needed an oil change, so on the recommendations of Lydia and Tanner, she took it to Gus Jenkins. Then she crossed the street to Lydia's shop. Opening the door, Erin gasped in shock at the mess. Merchandise lay scattered on the floor, as did the obviously damaged cash register. Shelves had been toppled, and Lydia was in tears.

"What happened? Was it a break-in?"

"Yes." Lydia wiped the wetness from her cheeks. "I already know of several things that are missing. Jewelry, a few paintings, but until I can clean it up, I don't know what else was taken. The cash register is ruined, and for nothing. I never leave money in there. I put it in the safe in the basement. I don't think they even went down there."

"What can I do to help? My car's in the shop across the street, so just tell me where to start," Erin offered.

***

They had made quite a bit of progress on the cleanup when Tanner came through the door. He jumped in and helped with some of the heavier items, like the shelves that had been overturned.

"Why would anyone just destroy this place? There's no profit in vandalizing your store," he commented.

"I think they were angry because the register was empty. This is my punishment for not leaving any money for them to steal," Lydia sneered. "I'm so glad that the shop is in town, so the city police have jurisdiction. With the mood I'm in, dealing with Deputy Kline would have pushed me over the edge."

"Any suspects?" Erin asked.

"Yeah. The jerk and his buddies. They've been hanging out across the street a lot lately, but this morning, they are nowhere to be seen."

"Who's the jerk, or need I ask?" Tanner wondered.

"Ollie. I don't know his last name," Lydia sighed. "I wish they'd send him to jail again. Or Timbuktu."

"His name is Simmons. So, the police are on this?"

"I called them first thing, They dusted for prints, but hey, it's a store. There are prints everywhere. We might get lucky, though. I wiped the register down before I left yesterday, and cleaned the glass jewelry displays. Yeah, we might get lucky."

The three friends washed their hands and locked the shop, then walked to the café for lunch. Lydia insisted on paying, as a thank-you for the help. Several locals had already heard about the break-in, and they expressed their hopes that the culprits would be caught.

"At least I have insurance and a couple of good friends to help clean it up," Lydia smiled. "Things could be a lot worse."

***

The next day, Lydia called Erin. "I just heard from the police chief. They got a match on the prints from the register. It was Ollie and one of his pals, the one they call Weasel. Their prints were in the system because they've both been in prison."

"So they're in jail now?"

"Yep. They picked them up a little while ago. They've been living in an abandoned barn out west of town. Weasel refused to talk, but Ollie made a deal. At first, he tried to blame it all on Weasel, but wound up pleading guilty to vandalism to get out of the breaking-and-entering charges, plus he violated parole. They got Weasel on parole violations, too. He'll have to serve out the rest of his original sentence. Seems he neglected to check in with his parole officer for several weeks. They're both going back to prison, so the town will get some relief, for a while, anyway."

***

Lieutenant Vince Sullivan strode through Cell Block A and stopped in front of a cell where a single person stood, staring between the bars. Sullivan had worked his way up the ladder from rookie guard to officer status over a period of about ten years. He was a bull of a man, with huge arms that bulged with muscle, short brown hair, and a uniform that was immaculate. His demeanor was cool and calm, and he seldom smiled while in the presence of inmates. On the rare occasions when he did smile, the effect brought a distinct chill to the air.

"Well, Simmons. I knew you'd be back. You just can't stay out of trouble, can you?"

Ollie Simmons sneered at the lieutenant. "We'll get you someday, Sullivan, when you least expect it. And I'll get out again, and when I do, I'm going to rape your sister and then I'm going to rape her little boy. I'm gonna make her watch while I slit his throat."

Sullivan stepped closer, and spoke softly. "I know that some of you jailbirds like to pee in a cup and throw it on your guards. And I know that some of you have AIDS, and a few other little illnesses.

Let me make it real clear to you, Simmons. I have the key to the gun case on the other side of that metal gate. If any of you throws piss on me, and I find out I got a disease from it, I will have nothing to lose. I will open that case and then I'll come through here and shoot every one of you and leave you to bleed out. And if *you* are the one who throws a cup of piss on me, I will shoot you in each foot, then each knee, then each shoulder, right before I shoot you in the gut. Don't mess with me, Simmons. As long as you're in here, I *own* you. Give me any trouble, any trouble at all, and you'll be sorry. You'll be *real* sorry."

Chapter 15
Mid-June

Two days later, Tanner knocked on Erin's door just after daybreak. She stumbled to the door in her pajamas, and rubbing her eyes, complained, "What in the world are you doing here at this hour?"

"There's news, and it's bad. Sit down and I'll tell you."

Erin shook her head. "I need coffee. Let's go to the kitchen. Do you want a cup?"

Tanner nodded, and while Erin started the coffee brewing, he began. "OPEC announced their decision this morning. They voted for a total embargo. They will not sell any oil at all to the US, and if any other nation buys from them, then sells to us, they'll shut them off, too."

Erin stared at him, stunned. "But can't we buy oil from Venezuela or somewhere?

"Venezuela is a member of OPEC. We can get some from Canada, and maybe from Norway, although production there is down. This is going to have a huge impact on our economy, so big that I can't even imagine it. But just think: if we had that pipeline from Canada that never got built, we could manage to get through this a lot better.

"Everything is going to get more expensive, everything from water bottles to toys to PVC pipe. All of our plastics and synthetic fabrics are petroleum-based. People are already starting to panic, They showed long lines at the gas pumps on the news this morning. Brazil won't sell us any oil, citing a fear of terrorism as their excuse. Norway's production is so far down that they don't have enough to sell us, or at least not enough to do any good. And the president was asked at a press conference if he would allow the government's oil reserves onto the market to ease the shortage, and he said no! His excuse was that we might need that fuel for the military if things go that far. I can't believe that he doesn't see what will happen if we can't get gas for all the trucks that deliver goods all over the country. And let's not forget that *he* blocked the building of the pipeline."

"So this is the poop hitting the fan." Erin wrapped her hands around her coffee mug. "Do you think that we'll get to the point of rioting and violence?"

"I know we will. I think that this is the proverbial last straw, and the camel's back is the US economy. I don't believe that the leaders of the OPEC nations realize that what they have done will cost them dearly, too. These days, every nation's economy is linked in intricate ways to every other nation's economy, directly or indirectly. The US is way too big to go down without the effects being felt all over the world."

***

The bad news continued to pour in for several days. A terrorist group claimed "credit" for blowing up the Alaska pipeline with explosives set at several places in remote areas. Safety valves prevented a huge spill, but small oil spills dotted the length of the pipeline. The damage would take months to repair under the best of circumstances. Someone also managed to use Stinger missiles to blow up many of the oil storage tanks in Cushing, Oklahoma, where a large portion of America's oil reserves were stored, and using plastic explosives, also damaged the pipes that had earned Cushing the title of "Pipeline Crossroads of the World".

Explosions and fires at refineries in Houston and Tulsa seriously damaged the nation's ability to turn crude oil into usable fuel. Electric power stations in California, upstate New York, and Texas were sabotaged as well, causing widespread outages. An attempt by hackers to get into the computer system for the grid was thwarted, barely in time to prevent a total shutdown of electricity for much of the country.

In response, a mob in Dearborn, Michigan attacked a Muslim neighborhood and killed dozens of people. It quickly became unsafe for any Muslim woman to go outside in a *burka* or a *hijab* anywhere in the U.S. Arab immigrants were bullied on the streets and threatened even in their homes; their children stayed home from school due to the taunting, shoving, hits, and kicks they received from classmates. If any American citizens tried to intervene, the mobs turned on them, too.

Within a few days, Tanner's prediction was proven to be correct. Reports on the news featured empty store shelves, videos of fighting at gas pumps, and looting in almost every city. The president made his usual "line in the sand" speech, and did nothing. Congress passed a resolution condemning the embargo; it was a useless gesture. In two separate incidents, one in Michigan and one in Illinois, tank trucks delivering gasoline to convenience stores were hijacked, the drivers beaten and left for dead. Most trucking companies simply recalled their trucks or told the drivers to park them and find a way home. Many truckers simply unhooked the trailers and took off, leaving whatever they were hauling for the looters. There was not enough gas available to deliver goods anymore.

Government policies having discouraged the use of coal, most homes and schools in the north used heating oil in the winter. Even though it was early summer, people were frantic in their fear of the cold that was only a few short months away. Hundreds of thousands of people got on waiting lists to have their vehicles modified to run on compressed natural gas, ultimately driving the price up for both the natural gas and the conversions.

At the time of the announcement, Mac McCoy was driving a tank truck from a refinery in Tulsa to convenience stores in McAlester. He heard the news reports on the radio, and simply exited the turnpike, headed toward home. Fortunately, he knew the backroads and was able to get there without traveling on major highways. When he arrived, he drove past the house, and turned onto a dirt track that led back through the woods to a large clearing where he could turn the rig around if necessary. He got several large camo nets out of a big plastic crate he had hidden back in the trees, and covered the truck with the netting. Then he walked home to his wife and child. He would come back later, and bring the fuel stabilizer he had stored in his garage.

***

Valerie's boss had already told his employees not to come to work until things settled down, but Valerie had learned just days ago that she passed her CPA exam, and she wanted to get her personal things from the office. She had already given notice, and was planning to start working for herself immediately. All that remained for her to do at her old job was to pack up her belongings and turn in her keys.

She taped the box closed and gave the office one last look to be sure she hadn't forgotten anything, then slung her purse over her shoulder and lifted the heavy box. Taking the elevator to the parking garage in the basement, she struggled to balance the box and open the car door at the same time. She heard a slight noise and turned her head just in time to see a fist coming at her. That was the last thing she remembered about that day.

***

Erin got the call from Jen late that afternoon.

"Val got mugged this morning. She's hurt, but not badly enough to be admitted to the hospital. They're full, anyway, with people who've been caught up in the riots. A guy knocked her down, grabbed her purse, and then kicked her, from what we can tell. She has two broken ribs, a big gash on her head, and is bruised pretty much all over. He also stole her car, but at least he didn't rape her. Things are really getting bad here. There's looting everywhere, and several buildings have been burned. Windows all over town are broken, and some store owners are standing guard over their shops with rifles. Sarah and I have been trying to get Valerie to leave town for a few weeks, but she refused. Now, she says she's ready."

"Then come on, and please be careful. Bring whatever you can't live without and get out of there," Erin urged. "Do you have enough gas to get here?"

"I bought a squeeze-pump thingie to syphon gas. We'll get what's in my car and use it to fill Sarah's Explorer. It should be plenty to get us there," Jen assured her. "We're all spending the night at my place, and we'll leave early tomorrow."

"What about your family? Are they coming, too? And Valerie's new boyfriend?"

"Mom insists that this will all blow over soon. She's convinced that we're overreacting, and Dad is humoring her. Valerie broke up with her guy last week. He was acting way too possessive."

"Well, tell them that they're welcome to come later if necessary. I wish they would come now. If it does blow over, they could always go back home, and no harm done. But I seriously doubt that this will just go away."

***

Tanner checked in with Erin later that day, to tell her that he was moving into his grandparents' house to help them and to be closer to her. So far, there was no looting or violence in Kanichi Springs, but there were rumors of trouble in nearby small towns.

Erin told him about Valerie and that the girls would be arriving the next morning.

"I'm taking three of my dogs with me, but I need to put some others somewhere. I can't leave them at the kennel if I am not going to be there to take care of them. If I bring a load of dog food, would you be willing to board two dogs for me? They're not as great as Blitz, but having them there would help keep you safe until your friends arrive."

"Of course, I'll take them. And just so you know, I'm staying close to home. If I do have to go anywhere, I'll take Blitz along and leave the other two to guard the lodge, but I plan to avoid going anywhere if possible, at least until the girls get here. Bring the dogs over anytime."

***

When Tanner got there, he let the two German shepherds out to run for a few minutes and unloaded several large bags of dog food. Erin had cleared a space for it in the mudroom, and Tanner stacked it against the wall.

"I have plenty more stored when you start to run low. I appreciate your help on this. The black dog is Flash, and the tan one is Major. They are both almost through with their training, so if you don't mind, I'll come over a few times and finish that here. You can even help, if you want to," Tanner suggested. "They're learning the same commands that Blitz knows."

Erin held her hands out for the dogs to sniff, then petted each of them. "Maybe I'll be able to sleep at night with them here."

"I'll be back tomorrow afternoon," Tanner promised, then gave her a quick kiss, and was gone.

***

Sarah, Jen, and Valerie got to the lodge just after 11:00 the next morning, Valerie was dopey from pain medication, so while Erin helped her into bed, the others started to unload Sarah's Explorer. Erin put Valerie in the second downstairs bedroom so she wouldn't have to climb the stairs, then helped carry in several boxes and bags.

"I'll need help with the big cooler, "Jen noted. "It's too big for one person."

"What's in there?" Erin asked.

"Whatever we had in our refrigerators. Some milk, meat, butter, cheese, and frozen veggies. We'll need to eat most of it real soon, before it spoils."

They lugged the cooler into the kitchen, and started putting the food into the refrigerator. When the cooler was empty, Erin stared at it, hands on her hips. "Next time, you need to get a cooler with wheels."

***

Just as they were clearing the lunch dishes, Tanner arrived on foot, carrying his bite suit. Erin made the introductions and invited the others to watch the training session. Valerie didn't feel up to going outside, and excused herself to lie down again.

With Tanner acting as agitator, Erin ran first Major, then Flash, through a series of commands, then worked all three dogs as a team. Sarah and Jen were impressed with the dogs and with Erin's new skill in handling them.

When the session was over, Erin offered drinks and cookies, so they all went inside, gave the dogs treats, and settled down in the living room.

"So, what's the plan now?" Jen wondered. "What do we do to stay busy around here?"

"Spoken like a true city girl," Erin teased. "There is so much to do, you won't believe it. I have a container garden on the deck upstairs, and there's plenty that you need to know to stay alive out here if things don't improve.

"If things get worse, there will be the possibility of others joining us. We need to figure out where to put them and how to divide up the workload. Every able-bodied person will have chores to do, and will most likely have to stand guard at times."

"Stand guard? Out here?" Sarah asked, incredulously.

"We're lucky to be so far from a large city," Tanner explained. "But eventually, desperate people will be fleeing the cities, on bicycles or on foot, if that's all they have. They'll be looking for food, shelter, and safety, and some will be willing to kill for it. People will lose their humanity, and do things they would never even consider doing under normal circumstances. It would be unwise, even now, to go outside unarmed. In a few weeks, it could get you killed."

"Do you really think it will get that bad in just a few weeks?" Sarah questioned.

"I do. It won't be the first time, either. It's happened before. There have been food riots in Amsterdam, Japan, India, and Poland. The riots that started the French Revolution began over food. Throughout history, when there is a shortage of food, or prices get too high, people riot. It's happened in Europe, in Argentina, anywhere that people can't get the food, water, and services that they depend on. Unless OPEC suddenly lifts the embargo, or we find another reliable fuel source, it's going to get a whole lot worse than you can imagine.

"For now, I suggest staying in as much as possible, learning all you can about survival, and staying alert at all times. Start training yourself now to notice your surroundings, and to trust your instincts. Maybe a solution will be found quickly, but I'm not betting on it. I think our way of life just changed and we had all better learn to adapt, or we will die." Tanner rubbed his forehead and looked at each of them. "Things are different now. Get it into your head, and don't forget it for a second."

Chapter 16
Early July

Over the next two weeks, the tomatoes on the deck began to ripen, and the girls were getting a quite a few squashes and lots of peppers. Each of Erin's three friends had read at least one of the books about survival or skills, and they had begun to adjust to a new routine.

"We need to wash the jars in really hot water. Valerie, would you start on that while I show Sarah an easy way to get the peels off these tomatoes?" Erin wiped the perspiration from her forehead. "When the first batch of plain tomatoes is in the canner, we'll make salsa out of the rest. Jen, if you would wash those squash, then grate them, we'll put two cups in each baggie and freeze it for squash bread."

With Valerie at least physically recovered from the mugging, all four of the friends were busy growing and preserving food, standing guard, and taking care of the dogs. Erin had already taught the others most of the commands that the dogs knew.

Tanner hiked over from his grandparents' nearly every day. On his advice, they moved Sarah's Explorer, parking it across the driveway where they could move it out of the way if necessary, but where it would block others from driving right up to the lodge. He used his chainsaw to cut a supply of firewood, and climbed up on the roof to check the solar panels.

"If I'm remembering correctly, Ernie said that the solar will produce enough electricity to run everything in the lodge except the dryer and the air conditioner, both of which draw down a lot of power when they start up, which would drain the batteries pretty fast. When the power goes off, you should probably hand-wash the dishes, too, just to be safe."

"So how are we supposed to dry our clothes?" Valerie snapped.

Tanner looked at her, frowning, for several long seconds, then calmly explained, "Valerie, things have changed. We are all going to have to learn to adjust to a new reality. Have you watched the news at all? Martial law was declared in New York, California, Florida, and twelve other states yesterday. Thousands have died in the rioting. All of the major cities are basically shut down. School isn't going to start this year, except in a few small, isolated towns, and maybe not there. Stores are empty and offices have sent workers home indefinitely, without pay, which really doesn't matter because the money is worthless now. The stock market had its worst day ever last week, and trading has been suspended for the foreseeable future. There is nobody driving on the highways, because there is no gas to be had.

"If you had stayed in Tulsa, you wouldn't be able to *wash* clothes, much less dry them. The water system is completely shut down there, as of two days ago. There is no food to buy anywhere. Hospitals are barely functioning because healthcare workers can't get to work, and there is a severe shortage of medicines. Hordes of refugees are leaving the cities on foot, walking out to the country because they think that farmers have food to sell, but the crops aren't ready yet, and the farmers don't have fuel for their tractors or other equipment. They can't even bale hay for their livestock.

"Police and other emergency responders aren't showing up to work. They're staying home to keep their families safe, or trying to get them out of the cities. It's a wonder that there's electric power anywhere, and it's only a matter of time before the workers that keep it flowing just walk away and let the power die. I've heard reports that rolling blackouts are occurring all over the country."

Tanner paused, staring at the floor, then looked at Valerie and added, "I'm sorry, but you need to accept that the life you led, the life you planned, is gone. You are so much better off than most people, because you have a safe place, food, water, and at least some electricity, and *you* didn't provide *any* of that for yourself. It's a gift from Erin and her uncle. Don't let what you've lost make you lose sight of what you still have."

"It's really bad, isn't it?" Jen asked softly. "I'm so worried about my parents and brothers. If water and electric services are gone, how long until phones stop working?"

"I'm surprised they've lasted this long. Do you know any ham radio operators near your parents' place? Call them and see if they know of any, before the phones die. Mac McCoy can help on this end," Tanner suggested.

"I'll call my folks right away. Maybe, with what's happening in Tulsa, they'll finally head this way. I know that Dad has some gas stored in the garden shed, probably enough to get here. If they'll come now, maybe we won't need to find someone to relay messages."

"I hope so," Tanner agreed, "Well, ladies, I need to go. Erin, will you walk me out?"

Erin rinsed and dried her hands and went out onto the front porch with him.

"I'm sorry," he murmured.

"For what?"

"For being harsh with Valerie. It wasn't my place to talk to her like that."

Erin laid her hand on Tanner's arm. "You didn't say anything that wasn't true or that I haven't thought about saying. Valerie is very intelligent, but everything has always been easy for her, until now. Her parents gave her anything money could buy. She's so used to having everything handed to her that I guess it's harder for her to accept what's happening. She needed to hear those things, so she can realize that this isn't going to go away, and that to live, she'll have to work for things she always took for granted before."

Just then, Tanner saw movement in the trees. He stiffened, and pushed Erin behind him, drawing his Kimber .45, but seconds later, Charlie came stumbling into the clearing and fell to his knees.

"Oh, no! Charlie, what happened?" Erin cried, as she and Tanner ran to help the old man into the house. His face was bloody and he was covered with ugly bruises and cuts.

"Them dang druggies from town caught me near ma shack. They wanted ma weed, said they knew that I must have some growin' out there somewhere. They beat me, and cut me up some, but I didn't tell 'em nuthin'," the old man vowed. "They want it to trade for hard drugs, but I ain't gonna let 'em have it. I think they would've killed me, 'cept they want me to keep growin' it for 'em, like a slave."

"Was it those punks who used to hang around with Ollie Simmons?" Tanner asked.

"Yeah, it was them. I was hopin' that with him in prison, they'd move on, but no such luck."

Tanner stayed long enough to get Charlie cleaned up and bandaged, then left with a promise to return the next day. Valerie moved upstairs to let Charlie have the downstairs bedroom, and gave him some of her leftover pain meds so he could sleep.

Jen called her parents and was able to talk them into leaving Tulsa, a decision made easier by roving gangs of thugs who were looting and burning homes only a mile or so from their house.

"We'll load up tonight and leave around 4:00 in the morning. Maybe we can slip away without attracting attention," BJ Martin told his daughter. "Are you sure there's room for all of us?"

"Erin says we'll make it work, Dad. I just want you out of there. You keep your gun handy, you hear?"

"Already planned on it. Mom has hers, too. We'll call when we get close and you can direct us to the lodge. Love you, honey."

***

Vince Sullivan leaned back in his chair and frowned at the list of guards who had not shown up to work the day shift. *We're dangerously shorthanded*, he thought, *and the natives are restless. Food deliveries aren't showing up. We have only a little water left in the tower and that's all the water we have, so no showers for the prisoners. The heat is getting bad and tempers are short. Maybe today would be a good day to confine the prisoners to their cells. The electronic openers for the cells aren't working, and I don't like it that the guards are having to use keys and manually open those doors, anyway. It'll be safer all around to keep 'em locked down.*

Before he could issue that order, however, a rookie guard got a little too close to a cell, and an inmate reached through as fast as a snake striking, grabbing the guard's collar and yanking hard, slamming the man's head against the bars. The inmate repeatedly jerked the poor rookie into the steel, until his body went limp. Kneeling and stretching to reach the guard's belt, the inmate grasped the keys to the cells.

Chapter 17
Early July

Charlie woke up a couple of hours later. His injuries turned out to be worse than originally thought. Two teeth were chipped and his nose was broken. Both eyes sported huge purplish-black shiners and one finger seemed to be dislocated. There was no doctor in Kanichi Springs, so Erin called the Fosters. They came over and Angie put Charlie's finger back in place, then stitched up the worst of the cuts and put on fresh bandages, giving him strict orders to rest for a few days.

Tanner arrived just as the Fosters were ready to leave, so they stayed for a few more minutes to share news and reaffirm that if things got dangerous, they would be in touch.

Jen's parents were due to arrive at any time, but when Jen tried to call their cell phones, there was no answer on either one. While Jen paced the floor, Erin got a call from Ian McClure.

"Erin, it's Ian. Tanner gave me your number. We've got serious problems here in McAlester and I need your help."

"What's wrong? You know I'll be happy to help in any way I can."

"My store was looted last night. Armed men and a few women broke the front windows and carried off everything they could. TVs, chairs, even a dining table. It's crazy here, and I am ready to get out. Tanner said you might have room for me."

"Oh, Ian. Are you okay? Were you there?"

"I was back in the office and heard the window shatter. I sneaked over to the office door and peeked out, but saw that I was outnumbered. There were at least ten or twelve of them. So, I slipped into the back room and prayed they wouldn't burn the place down with me in it. What they wanted with TVs at this point is beyond me. I am fine, but there's no point in sticking around now. And I haven't told you the worst yet." Ian paused as if searching for words. "There's been trouble over at the prison. Several of the guards just stopped showing up, I guess because their families needed protection, or they didn't have gas to get to work. They're real short-handed out there, and this morning, there was a riot. Some guards were killed and over a hundred prisoners escaped."

"Crap! It seems like the bad news just keeps on coming," Erin complained. "Ian, you're welcome to come here, but we are about to get close on beds. We have five here now, with four more on the way, and at least two families who may come later. I have some cots and sleeping bags we can use. We'll find room for everyone even if we have to make pallets on the floor."

"I have a full tank of gas in my delivery truck. I could fill the back up with mattresses if that would help."

"That would be perfect! Bring those, and if you can, bring sheets and blankets, too."

***

Ian arrived a few hours later with a truckload of mattresses, his clothes, a cooler of food from his house, and the tools from his garage. He also brought along a hitchhiker, and pulled Erin aside to explain.

"Erin, I hope you don't mind. Vince is an old friend. He saw the truck coming up the road and flagged me down. If it's going to be a problem, we'll just go find an abandoned house in town, but I can vouch for Vince. I've known him for twenty years, at least. As you can see from the uniform, he was a lieutenant at the prison, and he came this way looking for Ollie Simmons. Ollie made threats against Vince's sister and nephew, and when Vince went to check on them after the escape, they were both dead. Murdered. He has training and he knows a lot of the convicts on sight, so he'll be a good team member." Ian looked questioningly at Erin. "Can we stay?"

"Yes, as long as he knows that he'll be expected to pull his weight, I guess he can stay. I wish I had planted more veggies. We may run out of food at the rate the group is growing."

"He's a hunter, and we both fish. We'll be happy to help keep the group fed. Thanks, Erin. You won't regret it.

"We can store the extra mattresses in the truck until we need them. I brought all the sheets I have, some quilts my grandmother made, and a couple of sleeping bags. I figured the tools might come in handy at some point, too."

Erin looked thoughtful. "Let's park the truck to the left of the driveway, just inside the yard. I'm thinking that we're going to run out of room to park vehicles if we get many more, and they may give the bad guys something to hide behind while they shoot at us. I hate hearing about convicts on the loose. That means that we need to step up security around here."

Erin took Ian and Vince into the lodge and introduced them to everyone. "I think that what we have to do for now is have the two big rooms upstairs assigned to single men and single women. We will need to start conserving water immediately, so short showers, and only when absolutely necessary, and that means only when you're too dirty to stand it. The pump is solar, but if we run the well dry, we're in big trouble."

Everyone, even Valerie, agreed to be careful with water usage. Valerie's attitude had improved since Tanner's scolding. She was quieter than normal, but didn't complain and seemed to be trying hard to do her share of the work.

Jen was having a hard time controlling her nerves, because her folks were hours late and she still hadn't heard from them. Worry was etched on her usually smiling face, but she realized that there was little she could do except pray.

***

Two more days passed with no word from the Martins. Jen was barely holding herself together, and when Tanner came to check on Charlie, Jen asked him if he had any ideas about finding her family.

"Well, cell phones are still working, even if service is unreliable. I know some people who live up the turnpike, I'll call them and have them keep an eye out. Then I'll call a few others between Tulsa and here. They can put the word out, and Mac can get on his radio and see what he can learn."

"Can't we drive that way and look for them?" Jen begged.

"I'm sorry, but it would be a huge risk, with escaped prisoners in the area, nowhere to get gas if we need it, and not knowing if they're even still in their car. If they had car trouble, they may have taken off on foot through the woods, and we could pass them and not even know it. I wish there was more that we could do, but I think that the best thing is to wait and see if they show up. Now tell me what kind of car they drive, and give me a description of each of them."

Tanner made several calls and got commitments to watch for the car or anyone on foot matching the descriptions Jen had given him. One couple offered to ride their horses alongside the turnpike and search for any sign of the Martin family.

About two hours later, Tanner's phone rang. Some of his friends had found a car abandoned in a ditch about four miles west of the turnpike, and six miles north of the Kanichi Springs exit. Tanner put his phone on speaker so Jen could hear.

"Is there anything distinctive that could help us determine for sure if this is their car?" Tanner's friend asked.

"They have a tag on the front with a big bass. It says, 'I'd rather be fishing.' And there should be an OSU decal in the back window," Jen recalled. "Oh, and one fender has a dent in it, on the passenger side, I think."

"This is their car, I'm afraid, but there's no sign of your folks. And why would they be west of the turnpike? Kanichi Springs is way east. We'll keep looking for them and we'll let you know if we find anything."

"Thank you so much. I appreciate all your help." Jen said through her tears.

***

That evening, Erin called a meeting after dinner and everyone gathered in the living room. "We have to get organized about standing watch. I know that the dogs will alert us if they hear anything unusual, but there has to be at least one human, preferably two, awake at night to assess the threat and be ready to respond. If all of us are asleep, we won't be ready when we need to be."

Ian volunteered to set up a watch schedule, and Erin asked Sarah to plan meals, with Valerie and Jen as kitchen help. The men made plans to do some hunting and fishing to add to the food supply.

"I wanna stay here and help out, if that's okay," Charlie requested. "Them hoodlums who beat me up know where ma shack is, even if they don't know where the crop is. I'm feelin' better now, and I need to go get my stuff outta the shack and check on my plants. Then, if it's okay, can I join up with y'all?"

Erin gave the old man a smile and a quick nod. "Of course, Charlie."

"You're not going to the shack alone," Tanner insisted. "I'll go with you, and we'll take Major, too."

Charlie agreed, and added, "I'm gonna hit the hay. Been a long day for this ol' man. Goodnight, all."

Tanner turned to Erin and smiled. "There's no way I can make it back to my grandparents' before dark, and besides, the bears will be out, plus I'd just have to turn around and come back in the morning to go with Charlie. Do you mind if I stay?"

Erin laughed. "Of course not. You're over here helping us all the time. You're always welcome."

"Come sit on the porch with me. It seems like we never have time to relax lately."

"True. There's just a lot going on," Erin sighed as she led him out the front door. They sat down on a bench and Tanner put his arm around Erin's shoulders.

"There hasn't been much time for me to show you how I feel, to do the 'dating thing'. The way things are, I can't buy you candy or send you flowers. I can't take you to a movie or out to dinner. All I can do is help around here, provide you with dogs to protect you, and tell you that I love you, Erin Miller. I've loved you since the day we met, maybe even before that, looking at your picture and listening to Ernie brag about his beautiful, intelligent niece. I love you, and I want us to be together. I know the timing is terrible, with the country going nuts, but I want you to understand that this is it for me. You're the one, Erin, for always. I'm not trying to rush you. I just can't hold it in any longer. You don't have to say anything; I just wanted you to know."

"So much has happened in such a short time. I'm mixed up, and just trying to survive in this crazy world. My whole life had just been turned upside down, when suddenly, the whole world changed, too. Please, just give me a little more time. I'm getting there, but I'm not there yet. We both need to be sure, with absolutely no doubts."

"I don't have any doubts, but I can wait. In the meantime, I'm ready to help in any way you need, whatever I can do. My sisters and their families are at my grandparents' now, so I can be here as much as you want."

"Thank you, Tanner." And she kissed him.

***

With Tanner carrying his rifle, he and Charlie left just as the sun was coming up. Major ran ahead, but stayed in sight. Charlie's shack was about a half mile from the small clearing where he grew his marijuana crop.

As they approached the area, Tanner gave Major the hand signal to heel, and they moved in cautiously. The front door stood open, and they waited, listening for several minutes. Tanner then signaled for Major to search the shack. The big dog moved in, and came back almost immediately, tail wagging. Tanner then crept closer and peeked in through the dirty glass of the only window. There was nobody in the single room, so he waved Charlie in.

"Don't you trust the dog?" Charlie wanted to know.

"Yes, mostly. He hasn't completed his training for clearing a house yet, so I was just being safe. I'll stand out here while you grab what you need, then I'll help you carry it to Erin's. Hurry. Those guys could come back, and we want to be gone before that happens."

Charlie quickly packed his clothes, a couple of blankets, and what little food he had.

"Blast it all! They got my Glock. Those bastards! If I was smart, I woulda been carryin' it and wouldna taken a beatin'."

Charlie paused for a moment. "Oh, wait! They got the gun, but they didn't get the ammo. I hid it in this rusty cookie tin. I got some 9mm here. We'll take it, just to keep it from fallin' into the wrong hands. Maybe somebody at the lodge can use it."

"Ian carries a 9mm. He'll use it. You ready?"

Tanner took the heavy duffle bag and Charlie grabbed his backpack. Tanner signaled Major to come, and they headed back to the lodge.

"Let's take a slightly different route going back. We don't want to wear a path leading anyone to Erin's place. And any time we come back, we'll vary the way we travel," Tanner suggested.

"Can we swing by and check ma plants? I sure hope those punks didn't find 'em while I was laid up."

"Sure thing. Lead the way."

When they got to Charlie's clearing, there was no sign that anyone had been around. The plants looked healthy and bigger than the previous time Tanner had seen them.

"This here is Afghan Kush. I wanted to get some THC Bomb, but this is a reliable strain for this area, and it don't get too big for one person to harvest. I had to put it in this clearin' because it needs at least five hours of sun a day. The pH here is good, too, right at 6.7. I got a friend who's a barber, so I got him to save clippin's for me. I put a bunch of that human hair all around the plants every week, so the deer and rabbits stay away. Good thing we've had a little rain, or I'd have to carry water from the stream. Weed needs about an inch a week."

"When will it be ready?"

"Oh, around the end of September. When I harvest, you don't wanna be around. It stinks to high heaven, but it's worth it."

"Whatever you say, Charlie. Whatever you say."

***

About the time that Charlie and Tanner left the lodge, Richie Baxter was leaving Kanichi Springs with a load of prescription medicines and everything else he could pack up from his store. Rumors that several convicts were coming to Kanichi Springs had been flying around ever since the prison riots. Richie didn't know if the rumors were true, but he figured that one way or another, things were going to get scary soon, so he packed up all that he could fit in his Tahoe, and put the rest in an old enclosed trailer that he had bought from a neighbor a few months back. Towing the trailer, he set out to find Erin's place. Once he got outside of town, he called her.

"Hey, it's Richie. I had to bug out, and I'm on my way to you. Can you give me some general directions?"

Chapter 18
Third Week of July

Over the next several days, the group at the lodge settled into a new routine. Ian's schedule for the night watch worked out well, pairing each of the original three men with one of the women, for three-hour shifts, with Vince as a backup guard. He was still reeling from finding his sister and nephew with their throats slashed. They had both been sexually assaulted, and that convinced him that he knew who was responsible, since it was exactly what Ollie Simm had threatened.

Since Valerie was not experienced with any type of weapon, she was the only female who didn't stand guard, but Tanner and Ian were working with her on gun safety and had just started teaching her to shoot.

Every few days, they would take her at least a mile into the woods to practice, so the sound of gunfire would not attract attention to the lodge. Tanner knew of a place where the shots would echo through the mountains, making it difficult for anyone to accurately pinpoint where the shots came from. Valerie's reluctance to be around guns had vanished the day she was mugged, and she was eager to learn.

Erin and Jen were up on the deck one morning, picking green beans and watering tomatoes. Jen had been very quiet for days, sick with worry about her family. Erin had just reached down to pull a few yellow squashes, when they heard the dogs growling.

Grabbing the rifle she had propped against the railing, Erin gestured for Jen to follow, then led the way downstairs. Each of them had an assigned place to be, so that every approach to the lodge was covered. Jen's post was at the window across the living room from the door.

Tanner peered out the front window, carefully scanning the woods for any sign of movement. A flash of blue caught his eye; someone on foot was coming up the driveway. When the figure came completely into view, Tanner realized that it was Lydia, and she wasn't alone.

A middle-aged couple limped along behind her, the woman supporting the man, who seemed to be struggling. Tanner put a finger to his lips for silence, then beckoned to Jen. She quietly moved over to Tanner's position. He gestured toward the window.

"Anyone you know?" he whispered.

Jen leaned around to look, and blurted, "Oh, thank God! It's my parents!"

She started toward the door, but Tanner stopped her. "We need to wait. There may be someone else out there, with weapons pointed at them. Let's make sure that they are not being forced to act as bait before we open that door."

The three newcomers stepped onto the porch and Lydia knocked on the door, Waiting and watching, Tanner finally signaled Jen to step back and let him open the door.

"Come in, quickly," he urged, practically dragging Lydia inside. He helped the Martins, and as soon as they were inside, shut and bolted the door.

Jen held her parents tightly, as tears streamed down her face. When she was finally able to speak, her voice was hoarse and raspy, but the questions were rapid-fire.

"Are you okay? What happened? Where are the boys? Are you hurt?"

"Let us sit down and we'll fill you in," her mother begged. "We're exhausted and your father hurt his knee."

Everyone joined them in the living room, with Charlie watching the back door and Vince guarding the front. Erin got each of them a drink of water and put a pot of coffee on to brew.

Jen's dad insisted that he had only twisted his knee a little bit and would be fine as soon as he had some rest, so Jen got an ice pack out of the freezer, wrapped it in a small towel, and handed it to him before placing an ottoman where he could elevate the leg.

"We left Tulsa early, but didn't make it out of town before we ran into a roadblock," Jen's mom began. "They said that we were free to go, but young people between the ages of eighteen and twenty-five were being conscripted into a security force. They...they took our boys," she sobbed.

Jen's dad patted his wife's leg and continued the story. "They told us that the boys would be trained and assigned to a town in another state to keep people safe. They'll be fed and issued uniforms, but can't contact us until they complete their training and arrive at their assigned base. I think they take them to other states to discourage them from deserting and trying to get home."

Jen began to cry softly. "We've been so worried. How did you get separated from your car? Some friends of Tanner's found it a long way from here."

"We stopped on the turnpike to, uh, relieve ourselves, and three guys came by and carjacked us. They had the drop on us before we knew they were anywhere around. So, we set off walking. We slept in the woods, and went hungry. Then we finally got to Kanichi Springs, and found Lydia, who offered to bring us out here. She didn't have any gas for her car, so we walked." Jen's dad took a long drink of water. "Without her help, we would still be in town, trying to find a way to contact you."

"Where are your cell phones? I tried and tried to call you," Jen asked.

Her mother looked embarrassed. "We left them in the car, along with our guns. What a stupid, amateur mistake! I can promise you that we won't do *that* again. Now, aren't you going to introduce us to your friends?"

Jen introduced Tanner, Ian, Richie, Vince, and Charlie, adding, "You already know the rest. Guys, this is my mom and dad, Frances and BJ Martin."

Turning to Lydia, Erin asked, "How are things in town?"

"Lonely. A lot of people have left, mostly those able to walk to wherever they're going. I don't know where they went, but there's nothing left to stay for, really. There's no food to buy anywhere. Electric power is spotty now, and off more than it's on. The water treatment plant is shut down. People have gotten sick from drinking water from ponds and swimming pools. Several have died. I guess anyone who could get out just left. I was almost out of bottled water, and completely out of food."

"Then you'll stay here. You can't go back to town now. You're welcome here."

***

Charlie moved upstairs to the men's dorm so that Frances and BJ could have the other downstairs bedroom and be together. Lydia moved into the women's dorm with Sarah, Jen, and Valerie. *I'll have a room to myself for now,* Erin thought, *at least until more people show up.*

After a quick shower, BJ put on some clothes that Richie loaned him, and asked Tanner to come out to the porch with him.

"My wife is pretty upset about the boys. Do you think they'll be okay?"

"I'm not sure that 'okay' exists anymore, but if they have food and water, and are working with a group, they may be safer than we are here. It depends on where they wind up," Tanner replied, trying to be honest without being negative.

"I would go after them, if I could, but until we know where they are, there's nothing we can do, I guess. I hope that they can at least stay together, and aren't sent to one of the big cities. So, how did all of you wind up here?"

Tanner leaned back and explained. "I grew up in Kanichi Springs and I knew Erin's uncle. He was a friend of my family, and I've been checking in on the girls as often as I can, staying overnight lately to help with guard duty. Charlie is a fellow from town who's been living in an old shack in the woods near here, at least until he can harvest his plants. He grows a little patch of marijuana, but he's a good guy. He got jumped by some thugs, so Erin took him in."

Ian and I have been friends since we were toddlers. He helps me with my dog training and kennel sometimes, and I help him unload trucks of furniture for his store in McAlester whenever he needs me. There was trouble in McAlester. Ian's store got looted by a mob, so he came out here, too. On the way, he found Vince, who worked at the prison. He needed a place to stay, and we can use the help."

BJ looked around the clearing and chuckled. "Well, I guess this amounts to early retirement for me. Not exactly how I pictured it, but I am thankful to be alive."

***

Tanner left that afternoon to check on his family, walking through the woods almost soundlessly, as his grandfather had taught him. The soft snap of a twig breaking drew his attention to a meadow on his left, where a doe grazed. He saw bobcat prints and three squirrels, and made a mental note that he might need to add more meat to the larder soon.

Nearing his destination, Tanner stopped and surveyed the area. He heard the sounds of children playing, and that told him that his family was okay, so he crossed the yard and tapped lightly on the back door.

Rose lifted a corner of the curtain to make sure it was him, then unlocked the door and let him in. Talako followed close on Tanner's heels.

"I've been around since you stopped to admire that doe. You travel well in the forest, but you let me get close. Be careful, son. These are dangerous times."

Julia came into the room and hugged Tanner, smiling gently. She looked at her husband, then at her grandson. "You let this old man sneak up on you? For shame!" she teased.

Tanner patted his grandfather's shoulder and laughed. "He's the only one who has been able to do that since I was eight. I guess I know a better man when I see one."

Just then the twins threw themselves at Tanner, hugging him around the legs. "Uncle Tanner! Come see the pictures we colored!"

***

Talako, Julia, and Tanner sat on the porch later that night, talking about how the neighbors were doing and what was happening in the cities. Tanner told them what Lydia had said about the water being shut off, and people leaving town, and explained about Ian and

Vince joining the group, and how Richie had arrived with a full load of medications.

Talako frowned. "The only ham operator around here is Mac, as far as I know. Thank God that we have solar panels, but we need to start practicing light discipline. No lights from dusk until after the sun is up, unless we can blackout the windows."

"Yes, and we'll have to continue standing watch," Julia added. "We have only six adults here, so we're stretched thin."

"I can stay here more, if it will help. Vince is starting to come out of the stupor he was in over finding his sister and her boy. He can take my spot on the duty roster."

Talako scratched his chin, a habit he had when he was thinking. "We may take you up on that if things get any worse, but for now, you should stay at the lodge. You know, I believe I have a big roll of heavy black plastic in the garage. We could cover the windows, I suppose, in a room or two, so we could still use lights there. We'll need to really watch the children to make sure they don't reach for a light switch in the other rooms."

"It's already hard to keep them in sight and close to the house during the day. The older ones understand that something bad is going on, but the little ones want to play outside. They're noisy, too." Julia shook her head. "We need to do some drills or something to train them to get quiet, or to get down if there's danger. I hate to destroy their innocence, but they have to learn that life can be dangerous now."

"So, Tanner," Talako teased. "How are you doing in your quest to win the heart of fair Erin?"

Tanner laughed softly, shaking his head. "It's not a good time to court a lady, Grandfather. She has a houseful of people and the same problems we have, except there are no children there. Progress is slow, but she *is* warming to the idea."

Grinning, Talako winked at Julia and turned back to Tanner. "No, the timing could be a lot better, but I have faith in you. She's a beautiful young woman. Smart, too. You chose well."

***

Erin and Valerie were hanging laundry on two retractable clotheslines that Erin had found in the mudroom and Ian had installed across the patio, when Charlie spoke from the back door.

"There's news," he called.

Ian and BJ sat near an old radio that Charlie had found in the men's dorm. Television programming had gradually died out, and there was no longer any news to be seen on any channel, but some radio stations were still broadcasting. Reception was spotty, but the announcer's words could be made out if the volume was turned up high.

"Continuing riots at the state prison have resulted in the deaths of several guards and at least ninety inmates, but the remaining guards have lost control of the situation, and withdrawn to safety, allowing dozens more inmates to escape.

"Residents in the area are warned to stay indoors and lock all doors and windows. Many of the escapees are armed, and all are dangerous. If you are alone, please be advised that you should join with others in your neighborhood to establish a watch. Check on the elderly and avoid travel for any reason. Escapees will be looking for food, liquor, and clothing to replace their prison apparel."

Erin looked at Ian. "Would you mind moving the clothesline into the house? We'll let this load dry outside, then dry the rest inside. We probably don't need to be out in the open hanging laundry, and we need all clothes we have."

***

Tanner spent the night at his grandparents', but got up before dawn and showered quickly with a scent-killing body wash. He dressed in camouflage leafy-wear, then grabbed his PSE Dream Season compound bow, and a quiver full of ICS Hunter 340 arrows, tipped with Muzzy 125 three-blade broad-heads, and set out to find meat.

Moving silently through the woods, he carefully approached the tree stand that he had put up the previous fall. He hooked his bow and quiver to a line, put on his climbing harness and went quickly up the ladder. He then pulled the line up to retrieve his bow and arrows. Pulling his facemask on, he nocked an arrow and waited. The automatic feeder was empty, but a well-used game trail passed right in front of the stand.

Just minutes before the sun appeared, Tanner heard the faint sounds of a deer coming toward him. Only his eyes moved, as he tried to catch sight of the animal. It was a buck, a nice big one. The antlers were just nubs, due to the time of year, but the buck had a thick body. Tanner slowly raised his bow and started to draw, but heard another sound coming from behind him. He paused, and soon another, smaller deer entered the clearing.

The two bucks grazed a bit, lifting their heads occasionally to look around. One gradually moved over closer to the other. Tanner patiently waited for a clean shot. The smaller deer finally turned, quartering away. Tanner drew back the string, found the kill zone through the peep sight, and released the arrow. It hit the young buck just behind the shoulder, passing through. Both of the deer jumped at the sound of the string, and bolted away.

Tanner waited, listening, for almost 30 minutes. He lowered his bow and quiver to the ground, then climbed down and followed the blood trail. About fifty yards from the stand, he found the buck. He drew his knife and field-dressed the animal. *Thank you, Lord, for this bounty Oh, how my priorities have changed. Last fall, I would have shot the bigger buck, but now, I look for the best meat, not the biggest. This boy will be tender.* He hiked back to the house as quickly as he could, and borrowed his grandfather's Kill Shot game cart to retrieve his deer. Talako offered to walk back with him and help.

"This will be some fine eating for the family, and for Erin's group," Talako commented.

"Yes. It's a great blessing that I was able to get one today. We'll take him back to the house, skin him and cut him up, then I'll take some of the meat back to the lodge. Grandmother will want the skin. Can you help me hang him?"

"I'm old, not helpless," Talako replied.

***

For some reason that she could not explain, even to herself, Erin had not told anyone about the cave entrance in the pantry. The friends who were there were all trustworthy, she was sure, but she just hadn't mentioned it yet, even to Tanner.

Uncle Ernie had often cautioned her about loose talk, and all of his books contained similar warnings of the dangers that came from telling too much. But Erin had been thinking a lot, and decided that there was also a danger to the others, if for any reason she was unable to tell them about the cache of supplies, so she decided to tell Tanner and get his opinion when he returned.

He arrived later that afternoon, carrying a bag filled with venison, which Erin put in the refrigerator. They could cook some of it the next day, and make jerky out of the rest. When the others were all busy elsewhere, Erin asked Tanner to go to the upper deck with her. They sat on two overturned buckets and talked a bit about the prison break, his grandparents, and a few other things, then Erin was quiet for several minutes. Tanner could tell that she had something on her mind, so he simply waited.

"I need to tell you a secret, and then I need your advice. Uncle Ernie was big on prepping, you know."

Tanner nodded and grinned. "That's putting it mildly. He once told me that he wrote novels about prepping and instruction books about prepping, so he could pay for prepping. It was a way of life for him."

"Yes, it was. Did you know that he had plans to buy a few milk goats? He just didn't get it done before he got sick. I was going to fulfil his wish, but didn't find any before things went down.

"Anyway, he did more prepping than I knew, and had quite a large cache of supplies hidden. I'm the only one who knows where those supplies are, but what if something happens to me?"

Tanner looked thoughtful. "You're wondering who to trust, aren't you? I think you should consider it like this: if you trust people to live in your house and stand guard while you sleep, doesn't it follow that you can trust them to know where the food and bandages are?"

Erin sighed. "You're right. I just thought that if someone was captured by bad guys, they might give up the location to avoid being beaten or tortured. But the location of the cache is more than a supply room. It's also a place to hide out if we need to."

"Do you trust your friends? Ian? Charlie? Me? You have to be the one to decide, but I think you should tell someone, just in case. And if the group has to hide there, everyone will know then, anyway."

"Okay. For now, I'll just show you and Jen, and I will think about telling the others. Let's stay up after they go to bed tonight. You and Jen have guard duty tonight, but we can slip away for a few minutes."

***

By 9:30, everyone was yawning. The combination of working all day plus not having television or videos in the evening made them ready for sleep earlier. The Martins went to bed first, followed by Charlie. The others were not far behind. As soon as it got quiet upstairs, Erin got Jen and Tanner and led them to the pantry.

Jen looked puzzled. "What's going on? We're supposed to be standing watch, not hanging out in the pantry."

"Shhh. I need to show you something, but I am not ready to announce it to everyone. Uncle Ernie bought this lodge for a reason, and built this pantry onto the back of the kitchen to hide that reason. Here, take these flashlights, and I'll show you."

When Erin rolled the shelf out and exposed the opening, Jen gasped. "What in the world? A cave?"

"More than a cave. See where the floor has been smoothed, and notice those tool marks up high? Uncle Ernie had it enlarged so a grown man could walk through. Come on. There's more."

Erin led them down the slope to the cavern. Boxes, buckets, and tubs by the dozens came into view.

"This is Uncle Ernie's supply cache. I haven't had time to go through it all, but every container is labeled, and if he forgot anything, I can't figure out what it could be. There are guns, too, and enough ammo to supply a small army. And the cave continues through the mountain, with at least one other entrance.

"These caves are not only our supply depot; they're a place to hide, too, and they provide a secret passage to the outside. Tanner, I think the other entrance is near your grandparents' house. This could be a safer way for you to go when you visit them. I wonder if your grandfather knows about it.

"There's another branch of the cave that goes toward the west, and it may have an entrance, too. I don't know, but we need to explore it and see what's there. The time may come when we need an escape route, or a way to get back to the lodge safely from that direction."

***

Mac used his handheld to contact Tanner that evening. He had spent most of the day listening on his ham radio, but not saying much, just gathering news from different parts of the country. Tanner invited Mac and his family to come over for a visit.

Most of the group gathered around in the living room to hear what Mac had to say. He had heard stories from several places, including Atlanta, Tampa, Chicago, and Houston. Most of the big cities were extremely dangerous places to be, due to roving gangs who grew more violent every day.

"Folks in Houston are dealing with their usual hot, humid conditions, but now, of course, with no air conditioning. The heat is adding a new layer of meanness to the trouble there. The guy I talked to said that there are bodies lying in the streets. People just shoot you if you look at them funny. There's no food, the water has been off for a while, and there's sickness, too. He didn't know what it was, but from what he said, it sounds like cholera. All those dead bodies need to be buried for the sake of the living. Dead bodies are a breeding ground for disease, but nobody wants to take on the task of disposing of them.

"Chicago is a war zone. In spite of all their gun restrictions, it seems that there are an awful lot of guns there. Rival gangs have shootouts on almost a daily basis. There were two ham operators that I heard discussing the problems there, and it's about as bad as it can be. The government at least tried to send in troops to keep the peace, but they were outnumbered and didn't even make a dent in the violence. They reportedly fled when the gangs joined forces against them. As soon as the troops left, the gangs turned on each other again."

"What about Atlanta? I have cousins there," Lydia interjected.

"Atlanta's not as bad as Chicago, but large areas of the city are no-go zones. People are leaving on foot by the tens of thousands, headed to the country to find food, but there isn't enough food anywhere. Corporate farms are shut down by the lack of fuel for their big equipment. Small farms are able to grow crops the old-fashioned way, but not in the quantities that are needed. My contact there said that he heard of women and even young girls trying to trade sex for food or water. It's sad how few people were prepared for even a small crisis.

"The drought in California has killed off most of the fruit trees there. There's no way to get the fruit to people anyway. Many of the migrants who work on the farms have gone back to wherever they came from. The countries south of us must have been hurt by this because of losing us as customers for their goods, but at least they still can buy gas down there, if they have any money. They're doing better than we are."

"I wonder how things are in Europe and Asia. Without American markets, the Chinese must have a surplus of all sorts of products. They have a huge population, and if they've cut production because nobody's buying their stuff, a lot of people will be unemployed," Shane commented. "We bought a lot from Vietnam, Japan, and Taiwan, too. Any news from that part of the world?"

"Not yet, but if atmospherics are right, I might be able to get news from other parts of the world soon. It may be second or third hand, but I'll see what I can find out," Mac promised. "I also heard from some guys in Florida. Tampa is better off than some places. They're worried about hurricane season, because without the National Weather Service, they'll have a lot less warning about storms. And if one hits anywhere, the help that usually shows up won't be coming this time. They're on their own, not just in Florida, but anywhere prone to weather disasters or earthquakes."

Mac and Claire agreed to stay and share a meal with their friends, but made sure that they left in time to get home before dark. Little Kyra yawned, then waved goodbye to the friends who stood on the porch.

"I'm worried about them," Tanner sighed. "The baby is due soon, and their house is really close to the road. I wish they were back in the woods out of sight, just in case any bad guys come around."

"You're right. The plan is for them to come here if it gets dangerous, but Mac is pretty independent. Let's try to get them to come here before the baby comes. It'll just be safer for them to be with friends who can help. It would be good for Angie to be close at hand when the time comes, too."

"I'll talk to Mac. He loves his family, and I think he'll listen."

"I hope so. I really hope so," Erin murmured.

Chapter 19
Third Week of July

Tanner spent the night, and the next morning at breakfast, he seemed quiet and preoccupied. At the first opportunity, Erin took him aside and asked him if there was something bothering him.

"Nothing's wrong, but a couple of things have been on my mind. First, I have a lot of supplies and dog food stored at my facility, and we need to go get it. I also lie awake most of the night wondering where Ernie's other caches are. He was a firm believer in redundancy, so I think there must be at least one more somewhere. I suspect it's at his house in the Springs. It would probably be worth the gas to take Ian's delivery truck to town and see what we can find. With so many people here already, and more probably coming, we'll need all the supplies we can get."

"Just two of us?"

"No. I think it would be safer and faster for three, or even four of us. How about Ian, and maybe Sarah or Jen? If we find it, we'll load up all we can and store it under beds, or put it in the cavern or maybe another part of the cave system."

"Let's ask Sarah, so Jen can spend more time with her parents. When should we go?"

"How about now? The sooner, the better. I suppose we can leave the stuff at my place for a while. It's pretty isolated out there, but we need to get it sometime soon, before someone discovers it and it disappears."

"Uh-oh. I just remembered something. Ian's truck is full of mattresses and all the other stuff he brought." Erin sighed. "I guess we'll have to unload them and store them in the cave somewhere, but then, everyone will know about the cache."

"I have a better idea. There's room for a few in each bedroom, if we lean them up against the walls. It's not ideal, but it will work for now."

"Good idea. Let's do it."

Ian drove, with Tanner riding shotgun. Erin and Sarah rode in the back, and every bump in the road made a new bruise, but there just wasn't room for all four of them in the front. When they arrived at the house, Erin quickly unlocked the front door, then Tanner went into the garage and manually lifted the overhead door so Ian could back the truck right up to it.

Someone had already been inside the house. The back door had been kicked in, and the kitchen was ransacked. Whoever had done it seemed to have been after supplies. There was no vandalism; it was obvious that things had been taken, but nothing, other than the door, was broken or destroyed.

"Where would Ernie have hidden his preps?" Tanner mused. "It would be somewhere safe, where the temperature is fairly constant and there isn't excess moisture. That leaves out the attic."

"A basement?" Sarah asked.

"This house doesn't have a basement." Erin looked thoughtful. "Or does it?"

They began to search the house for supplies, or for any possible entrance to a hidden room or staircase. Once they had gone through the entire house, they met back in the kitchen.

"Is there a garden shed or something like that in the yard?" Ian asked.

They all moved to the back windows to look, but there was nothing at all in the backyard except a fence. When Erin turned from the window, she noticed a tall bookcase full of cookbooks. She stood staring at it for a moment, puzzled.

"That's funny. Uncle Ernie could cook basic meals pretty well, but he wasn't one to try out new recipes. I wonder why he had all those cookbooks."

She stepped over to the shelf and started pulling books out, stacking them on the dining table. Tanner caught on quickly, and started helping. Then he found the latch.

"Bingo! Erin, you're a genius!" The shelf rolled forward easily. "I think Ernie must have had a thing for hidden casters."

The opening revealed a staircase going down to a basement as large as the house. It was filled with the same types of tubs, buckets, and steel boxes as the cavern.

"Let's load up as much as possible, then close this up and replace the books. Hurry, before anyone comes," Ian urged. "When we come back, we'll only have to remove two or three books, now that we know where the latch is."

Tanner and Erin stayed in the basement, bringing items to the top of the stairs and stacking them for Sarah and Ian to load in the truck, so they wouldn't all be getting in each other's way on the stairs. Ian was an expert at packing things into a truck, so he got a lot loaded, while still leaving a space for Erin and Sarah to ride back there.

Chapter 20
Late July

Storing the new supplies under beds and wherever they could find space, they got the truck unloaded in a fairly short time. They had gotten quite a lot from Ernie's basement, but there was a lot more that they needed to get.

Erin seemed pensive that afternoon, and Tanner finally asked her why.

"I was just thinking. We have friends in town and we haven't checked in with them in almost a week. I am ashamed to say that I didn't think to drive by the Abbotts' house today while we were in town. I was too excited about trying to find Uncle Ernie's other cache. I haven't even talked to them lately. And then there's Gus. I don't know him well, but I like him. Could we try to find out how they're doing next time we go into town?"

"Of course. I need to see about Shane, too. I haven't worried about him because he can defend himself, but with the power and water off, he might need some help."

"Shane? Who's Shane?"

"Oh, I thought you'd met him. He's a martial arts instructor. American kenpo, which he affectionately calls 'break-a-head, break-a-leg karate.' He held classes here and also went to McAlester twice a week to teach there. I guess that's over now. I hope he's in Kanichi Springs, not McAlester. He's a seriously tough guy, but things are bad there," Tanner explained.

"Okay, so when do we go back to get the rest of the stuff from Uncle Ernie's basement? I'll call the Abbotts and see if they need anything."

"You can try to call, but don't be surprised or concerned if they don't answer. Our phones are still working okay, but we have solar power to recharge them. The Abbotts may not have a way to charge theirs. Let's plan on going back to town tomorrow."

***

Terri Abbott did answer her phone. She explained to Erin that Ernie had given them a combination solar/crank charger for Christmas.

"We're running low on food, but the worst problem is lack of water that's fit to drink. We've been putting a little bit of Clorox in rainwater that we caught in some barrels, but I'm worried. We're almost out of bleach, and if it doesn't rain again soon, we'll be out of water."

"We'll bring you some LifeStraws and some food tomorrow. You can drink out of a pond with one of those. You know that you can come stay at the lodge if things get too rough."

"Thanks, but Ken feels that we need to stay here and help folks if we can. We have some of the elderly people from town, and a few families with small children staying in the fellowship hall, and they need us. We'll see you tomorrow, Erin."

***

The next morning, when they turned onto the street in front of Ernie's house, Tanner spotted a small figure darting out the side gate. The figure ran across the street and down the sidewalk. Tanner jumped out of the truck and chased after the fugitive. His long legs caught up with the urchin halfway down the block.

"Micah? What were you doing at Ernie's?" Tanner demanded.

"I was just looking for food and medicine for Gus. He's hurt, and I'm taking care of him."

"Where are your foster parents?"

"Dead," the youngster hung his head and blinked back tears. "They got sick, bad sick. They ate some fish and I think it was spoiled. I didn't eat any, 'cause I don't like fish and there was still peanut butter. They died, so I went to stay with Gus."

"What's wrong with Gus? And where is he?" Tanner insisted.

"He's at his shop. He fell and I think his arm is broke. I'm not sure, but it's hurting and I wanted to find some medicine for him." Micah wrapped his arms across his stomach. "I didn't think it would be stealin' since Mr. Ernie is dead."

"Okay. We'll find something for the pain. You take it to Gus, and stay with him. We'll come to the shop and check on you in a while."

Tanner led Micah back to Ernie's, and explained to Erin that Gus needed medicine for pain. Erin ran into the house and got a bottle of pain pills from Ernie's stash. She instructed Micah to give Gus one tablet every four hours if he needed it, then sent him off to take care of his friend.

"I kept him out here so he wouldn't see the entry to the basement," Tanner explained.

"I figured as much. Let's go help get this truck loaded up, then we'll drop some supplies off at the Abbotts' and head over to check on Gus."

***

Ken Abbott saw the truck pull up in front of their house, and came out to meet them. He looked gaunt, having obviously lost several pounds. Erin had set aside food and other supplies to give them, but Ken was most excited to get the LifeStraws.

"Now, what are your plans, Ken? You know that you're welcome out at the lodge."

"Thanks, but we are going to stay in town for now. We're helping people who need assistance; in fact, the fellowship hall is almost full of elderly folks and single women who are afraid to stay in their homes. We have a few families here, too. Being together will make it easier for all of us. Safer, as well. There are only a few men still around, and they're here, too. Most of the single men and men with families left town already. I hope they're okay. We appreciate the help and the offer, but we'll be fine."

"I've been doing some hunting lately," Tanner said. "I guess deer season is now open all year, since there's no law enforcement in sight. I'll try to get a deer or a wild hog for you so you can feed all those people."

"Thanks, Tanner. It would be a huge help. Thankfully, there are a couple of gardeners staying here, and we're still getting some veggies out of their gardens. Pray for enough rain to keep things growing, and we'll have fruit to eat later, too. There are peach and apple trees in town. Maybe plums, too, I hope. Come by and check on us any time."

"We will," Erin promised. "And I brought you a radio, so when the cell phones quit working, we can maybe stay in touch. We'll probably have to climb to the top of my mountain to get good reception, but it's better than nothing."

***

When they got to the mechanic shop, Ian parked the truck, and waved at Micah, who was watching for them out the front window and ran over to unlock the door.

"Gus took a pill, and he's asleep now. Can you look at his arm? He's been hurtin' bad," Micah pleaded. The boy led them into the back room and up the stairs to a storage loft. Gus lay on a pallet of old blankets, sound asleep.

Tanner examined the arm that Micah indicated, and feeling the shoulder, gave a sigh of relief.

"It's not broken; the shoulder is dislocated. Ian, hold him on the other side, and I'll pop it back into place. It's a good thing he's out, because this is going to hurt. He'll be sore for a few days, but he'll be fine."

Gus stirred, then woke from the sharp pain of Tanner's efforts, but smiled a bit and said, "Ah, that's better," before drifting off again.

"Micah, we need you to stay here with Gus for now. We have a full load in the truck, and no room to take you with us this trip, but we'll come back and get you. You can both come stay out at my place. Stick close to Gus and don't be wandering off anywhere. We can't spend time or gas hunting you down, okay?" Erin urged.

"Okay, but do you have any food or water? We get awful thirsty."

Erin nodded to Ian, who ran out to the truck to get the requested items.

Tanner took Micah by the shoulders and looked him in the eye. "Now listen to me, Micah. Stay inside, away from the windows. Don't turn on any flashlights or light any candles after dark. Some bad men escaped from the prison, and they might come this way. We'll be back tomorrow and get you two to a better place, where there's food and water, and people to keep you safe. Just be really careful."

Micah nodded solemnly and promised to stay with Gus. He looked scared, but determined to take care of his friend. At only twelve years of age, Micah was already starting to learn how to be a man.

***

Early the next morning, Tanner, Ian, and Erin piled into the delivery truck and headed back to town. They planned to make one final stop by Ernie's house to get the last of the cache and grab anything useful from the main floor of the house.

"Okay, look for sheets, blankets, pillows, towels, shoes, jackets. Keep a lookout for flashlights, batteries, and guns, too. Grab anything that looks useful," Erin reminded them.

Like he had done at the lodge, Ernie had secreted several weapons in devious places around the house. Since Erin was familiar with the hidey-holes around the lodge, she looked for similar secret places, and found several. After about thirty minutes, they had gathered all the things that they could use, including the mattresses. Erin laid one mattress down for Gus and Micah to use on the way to the lodge, so they wouldn't get bruised up like she and Sarah had. Ian used ratchet straps to secure the load so it wouldn't fall, and had just started to close the back of the truck so they could go pick up their passengers at Gus's shop.

Erin had one foot raised to step into the truck when she suddenly froze. "Listen," she warned. "Do you hear it?"

"That's a motor, sounds like it's over on the next street. And it's coming this way," Ian exclaimed, holding the door and motioning for the girls to climb up. "Get in!"

Tanner got the truck started and drove toward the parking lot behind Lydia's shop. They locked the back of the truck, then Erin opened the back door of the shop with the key Lydia had given her. They slipped inside and began filling bags with essential oils, shampoo, lotions, candles, and disposable razors.

Ian jogged across the street and tapped on the door of Gus's shop. Gus was awake and had climbed down from the loft with Micah. He looked much better than he had the day before, but still favored his sore shoulder. Ian led them to the back room.

"There's somebody in town with the gas to drive around in a vehicle. It could be local folks, but it could be escapees, so we need to lie low until they're gone," Ian warned. "I'm going to stay out of sight, but take a peek out the front window and see if I can see anything. Stay here."

Ian slipped into the front section of the shop, staying low against the wall. He could hear loud voices as he got closer to the big overhead door, then he heard glass shattering. Taking a quick peek out the window, he saw several men across the street, breaking the windows of the liquor store.

Tanner and Erin also heard the commotion outside, and hastily ducked into the back room of Lydia's shop. They were trapped by the looters out front, and also by the fact that there were no windows in the back, so they couldn't see if it was safe to go out that way. From the voices they heard, they were also greatly outnumbered by whoever was outside.

Suddenly, Micah materialized beside them, grinning.

"Where'd you come from?" Erin squeaked, dropping the bags she was carrying.

"If you want out of here, follow me," he whispered, then led them to a narrow door in the corner of Lydia's back room, behind stacks of boxes.

"Come on, but watch your step," Micah murmured as he descended the stairs. He turned on a flashlight and guided them across a damp, musty basement to another door. "I found this when I was out looking for food. There's a tunnel that goes under the street to the empty building next to Gus's. He told me that these buildings are real old, and the man who built them put this tunnel in because he was a bootlegger, whatever that is."

At the end of the tunnel, they climbed a steep flight of rickety stairs, and emerged in the back room of the abandoned building. Sneaking a look across the street, Tanner patted Micah on the back.

"Kid, you just saved us. We'd have been in big trouble if you hadn't come. The looters are inside Lydia's shop now. Thanks for the rescue."

"We can go out the back and get to Gus," Micah decided. "He's probably wondering if we made it out."

Gus and Ian were relieved to see them, but concerned about where the bad guys would go next.

"There's at least a dozen of them, and I recognized two. Ollie Simmons and that little guy they call Weasel who follows him around. It's a good bet that all of those thugs are from the prison, since they're with Ollie. I think we should wait until they get done with their looting, then sneak over there and get out of town. I hate to leave the townspeople at the mercy of those hoodlums, but we can't fight them all right now."

"Let me see if I can get Ken on the radio and let him know so he can warn folks. I think most people are in the church building already." Erin paused for a few seconds. "Are we safer here, or should we go to the empty building next door?"

She left it to the guys to decide the answer to that, and stepped away to try to contact Ken.

The radio signal was weak, probably because they were inside a rock building, but Ken answered. As Erin described the scene downtown, he stopped her and she could hear him directing others to warn everyone about the convicts in town.

"Erin, I need to go. Thank you for warning us. Be safe, sister," and he was gone.

Erin stepped back over to the others and told them that she had gotten through. "So, are we staying here?"

Gus shook his head. "We should go next door. I've never liked that Ollie, and he knows it. When he was on trial the first time, I testified against him, so he hates me, and he might bust in here to get his revenge. He might even try to burn the place down, so we better go."

They turned to leave, but Gus and Micah lagged behind, stopping to pick up a couple of bags of their belongings.

Tanner, Ian, and Erin had just stepped out into the alley behind the shop, when suddenly, a man stepped out from behind a dumpster, pointing a large gun at them, and grinning.

"Well, now. You gents plannin' on keepin' that little gal all to yerselves? That's mighty narrow-minded. You boys just back up. Turn around and put your hands on that wall, high up. And spread them legs. Now!"

Staring hard at the man, Tanner caught a glimpse of movement behind the other dumpster. Then, shoulders slumped, he moved to obey. As he passed Erin, he whispered, "Play it up."

Bewilderment flashed momentarily in Erin's eyes, but she knew Tanner must have a plan of some kind. She smiled seductively at the gunman. "It's about time a real man showed up around here," she purred, running her hand down her side to emphasize her figure.

A flying foot seemed to come out of nowhere to kick the assailant in the throat. He dropped like a stone.

The owner of the foot grinned at Erin, then bent to retrieve the punk's gun. He called to Tanner, "Hey pal, how come I always seem to be saving your butt?"

Tanner strode over and grasped the man's hand. "Shane, I seem to recall bailing you out of trouble a time or ten."

"Yeah, I guess you have, at that."

Erin gulped. "Is…is that guy dead?"

"If he's not, he will be soon. It's kinda hard to breathe with a crushed windpipe."

Gus and Micah came out the door just then.

"We were only a few steps behind you, but we couldn't help. Sorry."

"No problem, Gus. Shane saved the day."

Shane nodded to Gus, then asked Tanner, "What have you all been up to in there?"

Tanner glanced at Erin, one eyebrow cocked as if to ask a question. She gave a slight nod.

"We were getting Gus and Micah out of town and to a safe place, but we got interrupted by some looters. You want to join us?"

Shane grinned. "Is there food? If so, count me in. I'm hungry. Where are we headed?"

"Out in the woods, to Erin's lodge, and we're taking the scenic route. Follow us."

They moved quietly over to the door of the empty building, and slipped inside, bolting the door behind them. They waited, listening to the yelling and cursing of the convicts as they moved down the street.

"We left all those bags of supplies in Lydia's back room. I hope they're still there." Erin muttered. "It's getting quieter over there. What are they doing?"

The day grew silent, then they heard an engine start. Tanner moved to the boarded-up front windows and found a narrow slit where he could see the street.

"They're all piling into an old van." He hesitated. "And they're leaving. Looks like they're headed out of town, but we couldn't be that lucky."

"Let's get out of here before they come back," Ian urged, starting for the door.

"Hey, Ian, how about we show you a trick?" Tanner joked. "Micah, lead the way."

Micah took them downstairs to the tunnel. Ian was shocked to learn of the secret passage. As they made their way under the street to Lydia's, he listened to Gus and Micah explain how it came to be built, and how Micah discovered it.

"I can't believe that I grew up in this town, playing and exploring in every nook and cranny for years, and never had a clue that this was here." Ian shook his head in amazement.

"I'm just glad that Micah knew about it. If not for him, those punks would have found us. I'm not afraid of a fight, but the odds were not in our favor," Tanner added.

Erin found the bags that they had left behind, right where they dropped them. "Hey, everybody grab a couple of these, please, and let's go home."

Chapter 21
Late July

That evening Jen and Tanner had guard duty, so after dinner, Erin put five flashlights on the dining table, then called a meeting for everyone else. They gathered in the living room, with the younger folks sitting on the floor or dragging chairs in from the dining room.

The story of the day's adventures in town had already been related over dinner. Micah had beamed when he received praise as the hero of the hour for saving Tanner and Erin from the bad guys.

Erin looked at each one of her new group members. The way that Micah had saved them by using the tunnel had made an impression on her. She realized that keeping the caves secret from the group was a dangerous decision that could cost them in an emergency, and she had changed her mind about keeping it from the others.

"I have a few things to tell you tonight. First, I was going to call Ken and Terri earlier. I tried my phone, and then Jen's, then Sarah's. The phones are dead. It was inevitable and expected, but that makes it even more important to let people know if you go outside of the lodge. From now on, nobody goes out without taking a handheld radio, especially if you are going to be out of sight of the lodge.

"Second, I hope that each of you will look on the rest of the group as family from now on. We have to stick together, and we have to take care of each other. What we saw in town today proves that one person alone does not have a chance against a gang of thugs. I'm afraid that what we saw today was only the beginning.

"Things are going to get worse, and we all need each other, so if you have a gripe or a problem with someone, work it out. If you do not want to completely commit to being a part of this group, say so now." She waited, making eye contact with each one, but nobody said a word. "Good.

"Now, there's something that you should know. My uncle was more than someone who wrote survival manuals and post-apocalyptic novels. He was a man who spent years preparing for a collapse.

"This lodge was part of that, as was his house in town. He bought this place because it's hard to find, but also because of one very special feature. Some of you grab one of these flashlights, and I'll show you."

***

Erin opened the entrance to the cave, and led the group through to the cavern. She pointed out the various types of containers and told them what was in each type.

"The food here won't last long with so many of us. That's why we have veggies growing in pots on the deck, and why we have to limit portion size. We'll also be canning as much as we're able this summer. There's clothing, too. Not every size, but Uncle Ernie bought yards of denim, fleece, cotton, and flannel, plus patterns for simple clothing in all sizes, even for baby clothes. There's a sewing machine in my room, an old Singer treadle, so I hope someone knows how to sew."

"I can do that," Frances Martin offered. "My mom had my grandmother's treadle, and she taught me how to use it. I sew pretty well, and I've been wondering what I could do to contribute."

"That's great. I can sew some, too, but right now, I'm busy growing food. Now, everyone, follow me." Erin took them across the cavern to the exit cave.

"This cave continues for a long way, all the way through the mountain. There is another exit, at least one. I have a map of the cave system, and everyone needs to get familiar with the way out. And someone needs to explore the caves to the west, through the exit on the other side of the cavern. We need to know if there is another entrance.

"If necessary, the caves will be a safe place to hide out for a while. That's another reason to conserve food. We may need to take refuge here, and the food stored in the cavern will be all we have."

Ian grinned. "Now I know why you wanted all those mattresses. We'll get busy in the morning and move them in here."

***

"You know, those caves seem to be beckoning to me. I can't stop thinking about the ones we haven't explored, wondering where they go, or if there are more caverns." Erin and Tanner were, as usual, the first ones up, except for Ian and Sarah, who were on guard duty.

Tanner glanced at her from the corner of his eye. "And you're looking for a partner to go off on an adventure with you."

"Well, not just any partner. It would help if he was tall and very handsome," Erin tilted her head and looked up at him, batting her eyelashes and smiling coyly in her best imitation of a simpering debutante.

Tanner laughed and nodded. "Let's go, then. That is, if you think I meet those qualifications."

"You'll do, I suppose." Erin couldn't hold back a chuckle any longer. "Oh, yes, I think you'll do."

While Tanner told Ian and Sarah where they were going, Erin packed some snacks and filled two canteens with water. Tanner took the backpack and Erin grabbed Ernie's map, a notebook, and a pen so she could draw what they found. She stuck a flashlight in her hip pocket and shrugged on a light jacket.

"Ready?" Tanner asked.

"Yep. And eager to see what's there."

The cave that they intended to investigate branched away from the northwest corner of the cavern, mostly toward the west. It was rougher than the caves they had already seen, with an abundance of rocks and pebbles on the floor, making it a challenge to navigate.

About thirty yards in, they had to stoop to get through a section with a low ceiling. They emerged in another cavern. It was large, but not as big as the cache cavern. The floor was sandy, with only a few rocks, and the walls were dry.

"This would make a wonderful place to set up as sleeping quarters if we need more room, or if we have to hide for a while. We could even store some of our supplies here." Erin turned slowly, examining the irregularly shaped space. "The cave continues over there, and there's an opening over on the other side, too. Let me sketch this out, then we'll go on."

While Erin added the new cavern to her map, Tanner walked the perimeter, shining his light into the smaller of the caves that Erin had pointed out.

"Hey, it looks like there's another small cavern through here," he told her.

Erin closed her notebook and joined him. "Can you squeeze through that opening? It's not very big."

"I think so. Do you want to go that way, or through the other one?"

"Let's go the other way. We'll come back to this one later if we have time."

They continued to explore that branch, which sloped uphill, sharply at times. Erin jotted down notes and drew all the twists and turns they encountered. Finally, they came around a bend and saw a light ahead.

Cautiously advancing, Tanner knelt and looked through the low opening. "I'll have to crawl to get through, but we need to see where we are."

He turned his flashlight off and dropped to all fours, creeping forward carefully until he could see out. Then he turned and signaled for Erin to follow.

A thick cluster of beech saplings grew right outside the cave entrance, providing camouflage for the dark hole.

Where do you think we are?" Erin wondered.

"I'm not sure. Let's see if we can figure it out."

Tanner took Erin's hand and led her around the beeches and to a narrow ledge where they could look down.

A small stream flowed past, far down the slope. Erin's eyes followed it upstream and she gasped.

"I know where we are! That stream is on the western edge of the property, and there," she pointed, "is the little pool that I showed the girls when they came to visit back in the early spring. We're pretty close to the road, too."

"This is great," Tanner decided. "We have three ways in and out so far, counting the pantry, and water available close by. How about we find a spot to sit down and relax while we eat a bite, then we'll go back to the new cavern. We'll still have time to check out that other cave, I think."

***

"We need to name these caverns. There are three so far, and it could get confusing. I already call the big one 'cache cavern.' There's another one in the east cave that has a seep and a small pool. I've been through that one all the way to the entrance, but didn't go outside. I had no idea where I was, and didn't want to wander around in the woods alone. We could call the cavern with the pool 'spa cavern' or 'the seep' or something. What could we call this new one?" Erin pondered, standing in the middle of the cavern in question.

"How about giving it a hotel name, since you thought of using it for a sleeping area? Maybe 'Miller Inn' or something like that."

"I know! We'll call it the 'west wing' for now. It's on the west side, and sort of oval, like the Oval Office, and that's easy to remember. And the one with the pool can be, oh, I don't know. What about 'the cabana'?"

"Sounds good to me. Let's go see what's through that other opening."

They entered the unexplored cave, and to their surprise, it also slanted upwards. About twenty yards in, it branched, and they took the branch on the left, which also curved to the left. Just short distance in, they found that it was a dead end, with just a small, high opening that would be a tight fit for a cat.

"Tanner, look." Erin's voice was full of apprehension as she pointed at the cave floor.

Tanner stepped closer, and saw the remains of an old campfire. Ashes and partially burnt sticks lay scattered, looking like they had been there for some time.

"Someone knew about this cave. Someone was here," Erin whispered. "The questions that arise from that are how long ago they were here, and whether they're still alive and in the area. If so, they could find our cache, and us."

Worried, the two returned to the point where the cave branched and entered the passage to the right. It sloped downward sharply, then leveled out, and was much longer than the other branch. A hairpin turn to the left, and the cave suddenly widened into a long, kidney-shaped cavern, about twelve feet wide and twice that in length. At the far end, they could see a light.

The opening to the outside was high, maybe five feet above the cave floor, but the wall was rugged and sloped, making it easy to climb up. Once Tanner had checked it out, they both climbed up and exited the cave, discovering that there was a large rock overhang sheltering a wide, level area low on the side of Erin's mountain. The opening to the cave was at the far eastern end of the overhang. They scrambled down the slope and stared through the trees, then turned to each other, grinning broadly.

Less than thirty yards away, beyond the wooded area where they stood, was a clearing, and in the clearing, they could see the white shape of a delivery truck. They could just make out the words painted on the side, 'McClure's Furniture', and past the truck, the lodge.

***

When they got back to the lodge, Tanner asked Ian and Shane if they would help him get the dog food and other preps from his training kennel. Erin heard them talking and wanted to go along, but Tanner didn't like the idea.

"Things are getting more dangerous every day, and I don't want to risk your safety. Besides, those bags of dog food are heavy and I doubt you could lift them."

"But I can load up the other supplies, can't I?"

"You could, but we can get it just as easily. Three can ride in the front of the truck, but if we have four, we'll have to leave a space in the back, so we won't be able to bring as much stuff. Please, stay here where you're safe."

Erin looked rebellious for a second, but then her shoulders sagged and she gave in. "Okay. I'll stay here, but you be careful, all of you. Take the backroads in or something. Just stay out of town. There are a lot more of those convicts than there are of you."

The three men got permission from Sarah to siphon gas from her Explorer and put it in the delivery van, then they headed for the kennel. They loaded over two thousand pounds of dry dog food and over a hundred cases of canned dog food, plus everything else they could fit into the back of the truck. There wasn't room for all of Tanner preps, so they hid the rest in a locked storage closet and hoped that it would still be there when they got around to coming back for it.

"Man, I had no idea you were so into prepping. You had a lot of supplies here," Shane remarked.

"Well, Erin insisted on paying me for Blitz, so I spent it all on preps. There's a lot more, too, hidden at my grandparents' place. We can get it later."

Unloading the truck went quickly, with Richie and the girls helping. The cache cavern was starting to get crowded, but they managed to fit the load in somehow. Tanner was concerned about rodents getting into the dog food, but Erin showed him some tubs of rat bait, which they scattered around on the floor of the cavern near the big bags of canine chow.

***

Rumbling thunder in the distance woke Erin before daylight the next day. She washed up and got dressed, then padded into the kitchen to make coffee.

Tanner moved soundlessly into the room and watched her for a few moments. The stress of the past few weeks was beginning to show on her lovely face.

"Good morning, beautiful," he whispered. She jumped, almost spilling her coffee, then smiled sleepily.

"It is a good morning, isn't it? I feel better now that everyone knows about the cavern. We have a fine bunch of people with us, and now the caves will provide security for any of us who need it, regardless of what happens to the others. What are your plans for the day?"

"I might go check on my family. Would you like to go?"

"I would love to. In fact, I'd like to go through the caves and see how close the other entrance is to their house. We should show them where it comes out so they can use it to come here if there's bad weather or they need a hide-out."

"I suspect it comes out very close to the property line, but we can find out for sure. I can't believe you've known about the caves for so long and haven't taken the time to explore them."

"I've been through to the end of the east cave. To be honest, Tanner, I was a little afraid that I might get lost or hurt checking them out by myself, and nobody would know where to look for me. I'm a bit of a chicken that way. I knew that the one on the east side must be safe, because Uncle Ernie said he had been that way, and he didn't mention any hazards. I only went as far as the opening, but I didn't venture outside alone. Taking unnecessary chances is a losing proposition these days."

"You're one of the bravest, calmest women I know. You have a valid point. Checking them out alone would have been foolish. We should tell whoever is on guard duty where we're going, just so they'll know."

Micah came downstairs just then, and wanted to know what they were planning.

"Can I go, too? Please?" he begged.

Tanner looked at Erin, who smiled and shrugged.

"Sure, you can go," Tanner assured him. "You'll get to meet my nephews. They're nine and ten, a little younger than you. We'll take Blitz, too. Do you have a jacket? It's cool in the caves."

Micah darted upstairs, then came running back, skidding to a stop in front of Tanner, and shrugging into a gray hoodie. They each grabbed a flashlight, and Erin led the way, at least when Blitz wasn't running ahead of them.

The portion of the cave beyond the cavern was new territory for Tanner and Micah. In some places, the walls were close, and in others, Tanner had to duck to keep from hitting his head. It was evident that Ernie had not had all of this section enlarged. The floor was rough and uneven, but not too bad.

Coming around a sharp bend, they could hear the sound of water flowing over rocks. As they continued forward, Erin stood back to watch as Tanner and Micah saw the little cavern for the first time. Tanner knelt and put his hand into the crystal-clear water.

"It's warm," he noted in surprise, then brought a handful up to his mouth and tasted it. "And sweet, too! This is fantastic. Ernie picked the perfect piece of property when he bought this place. See, the pool must have an outlet somewhere, because even with water coming in, the pool doesn't overflow."

Micah looked puzzled. "And that's good?"

"Yes, it's very good. It means that the pool probably won't ever flood the caves, and the water isn't stagnant, so we can use it. If we bathe in it, the pool will naturally cleanse itself. We can drink the water from the seep, too. We probably should filter it just to be safe, but if we ever do have to live in the caves, we'll have a water source without having to go outside."

They passed through to the other side of the cavern, and again, the cave narrowed somewhat, to the point that the adults had to turn sideways to get through. It was impossible to estimate how far they had come, since the cave had many turns, but they eventually reached the opening to the outside.

A slender shaft of dappled sunlight illuminated the cave's door to the outside world. Tanner extended an arm to stop Micah from running out, cautioning him and Erin to be quiet. He silently

131

moved forward, staying in the shadows as much as possible. He listened for several minutes, peering around, then finally slipped out, checking the area. There was no sound other than that of birds twittering and the light breeze fluttering the leaves.

Tanner beckoned, and the others joined him, blinking in the light. The storm had passed to the north, and the ground was dry. Most of the sky was bright blue, and it was a beautiful day.

"Look at how the angle of that rock conceals the entrance from that side, and that thick clump of trees does the same on the other." Erin stepped a few yards away, and looked back. "It makes the opening really hard to see unless you know it's there. If we had tried to find this from the outside, I doubt that we could have done it. So, Tanner, where do you think we are in relation to your grandparents' house?"

Tanner rubbed his chin, looking around. "I played in these woods for years with my sisters and cousins, and never knew that this cave was here. The house is right down there," he said, gesturing to the northeast. "It's very close, just fifty or sixty yards."

***

They made their way down the slope, with Tanner giving Micah a lesson on how to move quietly through the woods. As they approached the house, Talako and Julia stepped out on the porch to greet them.

"How did you know we were coming?" Micah wanted to know.

"We have three of Tanner's dogs in the house. They went on alert, so we did, too." Talako ruffled the boy's hair. "How are you, Micah? Come in the house, and meet our grandchildren."

After introductions were made, Zeke immediately invited Micah to join a game the children were playing in another room. Blitz eagerly tagged along, leaving the adults to visit. Julia served tea, and they chatted about the weather and their gardens for a few minutes, then Tanner turned to his grandfather.

"Did you know about the cave up the slope about fifty yards or so?"

Talako laughed. "Of course. It's not on my property, but I knew of it. Ernie showed the caves to me, and I helped him design and build the pantry and its hidden doorway. That pantry isn't original to the house. We did a good job adding it on without it *looking* like it was added on, didn't we?"

Tanner gave him an exasperated look. "And you never mentioned it?"

Talako shrugged. "Ernie swore me to secrecy. It was not my secret to reveal. I knew that he thought Erin was curious enough to look, and smart enough to figure it out. In case she didn't, I would have told her soon."

Erin touched the old man's arm. "Talako, Julia, if things get worse and you need to leave this house, you are all welcome to use the cave to come to us at the lodge. It'll be crowded, but we'll make it work."

"Thank you, Erin. We'll keep that in mind, and we appreciate it, especially since we have children here. We don't plan on taking any chances with their safety," Julia assured her.

Then Tanner and Erin told them about the trouble in town, describing their narrow escape, and how Micah used the secret tunnel to save them. They told about Richie coming out with all the medicines and supplies from his store, and about retrieving all the preps that Ernie had left in his house.

Julia frowned thoughtfully. "There is evil in the world, and I do not believe that our God wants us to sit back and not defend our families. Killing in self-defense or in the defense of others is not murder. Those who commit acts of evil must be stopped."

Tanner nodded in agreement. "I hope sometimes that they'll move on, but if they don't, we'll have to deal with them. There are innocent people in town, who are struggling to survive even without the menace the convicts bring. There will be a day of reckoning, and I plan to be there."

"But if they move on," Talako interjected, "they'll just hurt people in some other town. We know what kind of men they are. It would be wrong to allow them to continue to rape, steal, and kill, moving from town to town, maybe growing in number as other evil men or women join them. We don't have an efficient way to warn the other towns, because we don't know where they might go next and we have no phones now to call a warning."

The old man shook his head. "No, we should deal with them here, if possible. If it turns out that they have already left our town, we should get Mac to warn any ham operators in the area."

"I left a hand-held radio with the preacher," Erin remembered. "We can communicate with him, if we go up near the top of the mountain. Many of the women and elderly are already staying at the church building."

"Good thinking, Erin. If you have to go into town to help them, I'll go with you, and so will John and Will, I'm sure." Talako offered.

Erin expected Julia to protest, but the old woman just smiled serenely. "He's an old man, but he is also a formidable warrior. If our friends need help, I would expect no less of him."

Chapter 22
Late July

As soon as they got back to the lodge, Erin made sure that all the hand-held radios from the cache were charged. She used solar chargers and placed them on the deck, so they would get full sun for the rest of the day. There were enough for everyone, and she made it clear that everyone was to keep one clipped to a belt or pocket, or beside the bed, at all times.

Tanner took one that had a full charge and tried to contact Ken. He went outside and began climbing the mountain, trying to find a spot where he could get through. After several attempts, he found a place where he had adequate reception.

"Had any more trouble there?" Tanner inquired.

"Not much at our location, but a young woman was gang-raped yesterday on the other side of the park. They killed her, Tanner. We found her body less than an hour ago. And they beat up an old couple who lived behind the grocery store. The woman is with us now, but the man didn't make it. He died on the way here. We've been trying to gather in as many people as we can, but finding that girl, and those old folks, has really brought home to me that we are in over our heads.

"Those punks are getting more brazen every day, like they think they own the whole town, and we don't have enough weapons to defend ourselves if they come here."

"You're armed?" There was a hint of surprise in Tanner's voice.

"I am, and so are a few of the men who are still here. Most of the population has left already, but there are four able-bodied men here with us. They brought their families here for safety.

" Some folks have been critical of me for allowing guns in the church building and for carrying one myself, but I can't stand by and let them hurt people. I don't believe the Lord wants me to, either. I think he knows the difference between defense of the innocent and just killing someone. I can't let those convicts hurt my family or my friends. The Lord is my judge, and I will face Him someday, able to hold my head up and say that I stood for the weak.

"He knows my heart, and He knows the hearts of those thugs. I will *not* kill except to protect others, but I will do what is necessary if they come here."

"I understand, Ken. We've been talking about this. Keep gathering all the townspeople that will come, and warn those who won't come to stay inside their homes. I'll get back to you, but I believe help is on the way. I won't say more than that on an open radio frequency, but I'll be in touch."

***

Tanner went in search of Erin, finding her on the deck, checking her plants. "We need to open the long canisters in the cavern. It looks like there's a war about to start in town, and if I'm not mistaken, there are rifles in those canisters."

Erin arched an eyebrow. "I believe you're right about the canisters. At least, that's what the labels on them say. Let's go open them up. Grab one of the guys, and we'll unload what you think we will need. I don't know why I haven't opened them before, except that there was no urgent need, and in the canisters, they stay clean and dry."

On the way to the pantry, they ran across Shane, and Tanner asked if he was busy,

"Nope, not at the moment. You need me?" Shane offered.

"Come on, we have a little chore to do that you might find interesting. Let me grab a couple of screwdrivers. I'll meet you in the pantry."

Erin led Shane through to the cavern, where Tanner joined them a few minutes later. Each canister had six screws holding the lid down tight, so Tanner and Shane got to work opening them. Tanner got his open first, and pulled out a Remington 700 BDL 270. There were three more just like it in the giant canister, wrapped in padding to keep them from banging against each other. Shane's canister contained the same thing, and there were more canisters to open.

"There are some smaller canisters over here. They are full of Glock 21s, and there's ammo, enough to fight a small war. Those containers over there have the scopes for the rifles. They'll have to be mounted and sighted in. Uncle Ernie had the money to buy what he thought we would need, and he didn't skimp. I think the scopes are Leupold." Erin looked around and found what she was looking for. "And these two canisters have Glock 9mm for those who can't handle a .45, so Valerie and Frances might need those."

"Valerie and Frances *will* need them, but not for the fight in town that's coming. They'll be staying here at the lodge." Tanner held up one of the rifles. "These guns look brand new. They've been cleaned and packed away carefully, so they didn't collect dust or moisture. They'll be ready to go as soon as we can get the scopes on them. We'll go to the spot where we've been teaching Valerie to shoot, and get them sighted in. Tomorrow morning, I want to have a meeting with all of our bunch, plus my grandfather, Will and John, the Fosters, Mac, and maybe Jimmy Gibbs. We are going to protect our friends in town, and that gang of convicts is going to find out that they do *not* own Kanichi Springs."

***

Tanner used his radio to contact their neighbors and his grandfather. All of them agreed to meet at the lodge early the next morning.

As dawn painted the sky bright orange, peach, and dark blue, the neighbors began to arrive. Nolan's older son, Paul, came with his dad. Jimmy brought his twenty-year-old twins, Hunter and Heather.

Charlie and Gus carried in chairs from the patio and the dining room, but even then, most of the group had to sit on the floor or the hearth. BJ, Frances, and Valerie volunteered to stand watch so the others could attend the meeting.

Tanner began by describing what they had witnessed in town, then told them what he had heard from Ken.

"These men are convicted criminals who have shown that they have no intention of trying to live like civilized people. They have looted and destroyed property, and now, they've raped and killed. They are animals, and it's up to us to stop them."

Jimmy Gibbs asked, "So what do you plan to do, and when?"

"Kill them, as soon as we can," Gus interjected.

Voices erupted throughout the room, expressing either agreement or concerns. Tanner gave Ian a look and a nod, which resulted in Ian giving a loud, shrill whistle. The silence was instantaneous. "Calm down, folks! When everyone talks, nobody is heard. Let's discuss this calmly," Ian urged.

Charlie spoke up before anyone else could say anything. "Most folks think I'm just an ol' hippie pothead, but I got some thoughts on this. First of all, let's say we managed to take some of them scumbags alive, which ain't likely, because they're gonna fight back hard. What can we do with 'em?

"Give 'em a talkin' to and let 'em go? Take 'em outta town and dump 'em? If we do that, they'll either come back here lookin' fer revenge, or go hurt folks in some other town. So, do we put 'em in jail? Nobody's laid eyes on the town's cops in several weeks. The jail here only has two cells, and who would guard 'em? And we sure don't want to have to feed 'em ferever. Food is in short supply as it is. They sure cain't go back to the prison, because there ain't nobody there to watch 'em, either. No other town is gonna take 'em off our hands, and we'll get no help from that idiot Deputy Kline. Ain't nobody seen him around lately, anyway.

"I say if we catch any alive, we have us a trial, and if they're found guilty, we execute 'em. It's the only way that makes any sense."

Gus grinned. "Charlie, that's the longest speech I ever heard from you in the sixty years I've known you." A few people chuckled.

Tanner looked around at his friends and neighbors. Charlie's little speech had them thinking, and the room grew quiet.

Finally, Tanner broke the silence. "Does anyone have a viable alternative? Speak up now if you do."

Vince was leaning against the railing of the spiral staircase, but straightened and stepped forward. "I worked Cell Block A at the prison. There was no inmate on that cell block who had not committed a violent crime. Rape, assault, murder, armed robbery, kidnapping, and *some* of them could check 'all of the above' for those crimes. Those cells were filled with the worst of the worst, and I am ashamed to admit that most of the ones who escaped were from my cell block. It doesn't matter that they escaped while we were shorthanded. I bear the responsibility because the guards I trained did not stand firm. If those inmates are now terrorizing your town, I say it's time to put a permanent stop to it."

Nolan stood up, a determined look on his face. "This state has the death penalty for those a jury says are guilty of premeditated murder. Since the prisons can't take robbers, rapists, and looters anymore, those crimes might need to be punishable by death, too. Those convicts have committed all sorts of serious crimes. Like in the days of the Wild West, when stealing a man's horse would get you hung from the nearest tree because it endangered the man's life to be without a horse, stealing food and supplies endangers lives today.

"Government courts are not able to do the job right now, so that means that we citizens have to do it ourselves. I say Charlie's right; we need to fight these men, because they have killed and raped in our town. If any survive, we have a trial, and like Charlie said, we execute those found guilty."

Tanner quickly jumped in. "All in favor, raise your right hand."

Several hands shot up immediately. Others were raised more slowly, but every hand went up.

"Okay," Tanner asserted. "Now we need a plan. There's work to do. Who knows how to mount a scope on a rifle? Who has military experience?"

"Charlie, Mac, John, Gus, Nolan, and I are veterans, but Nolan has the most experience with planning an operation like this. Vince knows those punks, so he should have input, too," Talako answered. "How about the seven of us go sit on the porch and see what we can come up with?"

"Great," Tanner agreed. "Ian, Shane, Will, Erin, and I will work on those scopes. Sarah, could you find some markers and paper? Get someone to help you, and draw us some targets? We'll need a lot, since we need to sight these rifles in."

"I can help with scopes, too," Jen offered. "I've been hunting since I was nine, and Dad taught me to do whatever needed doing. He could help, too, if someone would relieve him. He's on guard duty."

"Richie!" Tanner called. "Can you handle a gun?"

"Yes. I'm not so good with a handgun, but I can shoot a squirrel in the head at a hundred yards with a rifle. Will that be good enough?"

"Yep, that'll do it. Please relieve BJ so he can help mount scopes. He's probably ready to sit down for a while, anyway. Jimmy, Hunter, Heather – help out wherever you can."

The lodge grew quiet as they all settled in to work on their assigned tasks. Even Micah joined in, helping Sarah, Valerie, and Frances draw circles on sheets of paper. That job went quickly, so after making several targets each, Valerie and Frances went to the kitchen to make soup for lunch. They used meat from Tanner's buck and veggies from Erin's container garden on the deck, and soon the aroma filled the lodge.

By the time everyone else had finished a bowl of soup, most of the rifles had scopes, so Tanner's group took a quick break to eat. Sarah had a stack of about 60 targets ready to go. The men who were discussing a plan for the coming battle were still working on strategy, so several of those who could shoot hiked to the valley where Tanner and Ian had been teaching Valerie. It took a while, but they got enough of the rifles sighted in for everyone in the group, then carried them carefully back to the lodge.

Talako and the other military men were waiting for them when they got back. The veterans had come up with a scheme to take back the town. They had chosen Nolan to be in command, since he had extensive experience and was also the most physically fit.

"Because of their inexperience with weapons, we have decided that Valerie and Frances will stay at the lodge. Angie will also be here, and those three will prepare to receive wounded. BJ, Richie, and Mac will stay behind to provide security for the lodge. We could sure use Mac in town, but he's got a wife who's eight months pregnant, so he stays here. Micah, you'll also stay here to help out, as will Paul." Nolan glanced at his eldest. "Sorry, son, but we need you here. You can help your mother set up in case we have casualties.

"Now we all know that no plan survives contact with the enemy, but here's one that has a real good chance of working. From what we can tell, that gang has looted just about all of the stores in town, so we figure they'll start scavenging in homes next. Since there are three small neighborhoods where just about everyone in town lives, we will split into three squads to cover those neighborhoods. Each squad's position will allow them to see not only their own area, but also to have good visuals on at least one other squad's area.

"Squad leaders will be Gus, Talako, and John. Charlie was a sniper in Vietnam, so he is going to be up in the steeple of the church. That's the highest spot in town, with a decent view of almost everything. Plus, he can help protect the people who have taken refuge there. The squad assigned to that part of town will also be larger than the other squads, because they not only have to watch that neighborhood, they have to guard the church. As far as we know, only a few of the men inside the church are armed, so keeping those people safe is a priority. Hopefully, the gang will come into town from the west, the end furthest from the church, and we can stop them before they get near the church, but we can't take that for granted.

"Every person will have a radio, and we will use code names for the squads, and for Nolan and Charlie. Each of you will have both a rifle and a handgun, and each squad will have at least one person with binoculars. Now, we'll break up into squads and let your leaders tell you the specifics of the plan."

***

Before dawn the next morning, the three squads were in place. Talako's squad was designated Gray Eagle, and was the larger squad assigned to the area around the church building. Charlie climbed up and through a trap door that gave access to the tiny observation platform in the steeple. It made a perfect spot for the old sniper to set up. His call sign was Hawkeye.

Shane's code name was Lone Eagle, and he was in the middle of downtown on the ground level so he could stay mobile. His quickness in assessing threats paired with his fighting skills, both with weapons and hand-to-hand, made him a valuable asset. His assignment was to move quickly to wherever the gang got out of their van, and take whatever action he deemed appropriate at the time.

The men who were already in the church building guarded the outside doors. Ken and Sarah guarded the stairway to the basement, where the women and children were, in case anyone got that far. Heather and Jimmy were in the classrooms upstairs, overlooking the street and parking lot. Talako took up his position in an empty house across the street, and Nolan, code named Blue Eagle, was in an upstairs window of a house across the parking lot from the church. They both had a clear view of the entire street, and Talako's position allowed him to see most of downtown, as well as the small cluster of houses on the street behind Lydia's shop.

Gus's squad, Green Eagle, was assigned to the downtown area. From their spot on the roof of an abandoned store, Gus and Hunter could help Talako cover the homes behind Lydia's, while Tanner and Erin were on the roof of Gus's shop. Tanner watched the alley behind the shop and the homes on the next street. Erin had the front, and was expected to see the gang first if they came from the west, the direction they had gone when they left town. Erin's position was designated Aerie One.

Red Eagle, John's squad, had the southeast section of town, and were able to see the homes there, as well as monitor the road that led out of town to the south. Will and Vince could see the east end of Main Street and the intersection near the church. John and Ian were on the roof of the old feed store, the last building at that end of town, and their position was called Aerie One.

Each squad had an assigned channel to communicate within the squad, and Nolan had his own channel as commander. He had instructed one of each pair of fighters to stay tuned to the squad channel, and the other to stay on his channel, to speed up communications. Charlie and Shane would monitor Nolan's channel.

Everyone was ready to move if needed elsewhere, except those guarding the church. They had a lot innocent people there to protect, and they all considered that protection to be paramount. After all, keeping the townspeople safe was the ultimate goal, the main reason they were there, ready to fight.

***

The wait seemed interminable, and those who were on roofs began to feel the heat of the blazing sun soon after it rose. There was not even a wisp of a breeze. Erin wiped the perspiration from her forehead, and with the sun at her back, used her binoculars to scan to the west, past the buildings of town, down the two-lane highway that connected the town to the turnpike. She supposed that the bad guys were sleeping off a drunk, and would be late coming into town.

As time dragged on, everyone got sweaty and tense from the waiting, but Erin continued to watch the highway. Suddenly, she caught a tiny flash of light, a reflection from the sun on something shiny, then she heard the faint hum of an engine, just a split second before she saw the beat-up old van top a hill in the distance.

"Blue Eagle, Blue Eagle. This is Green Eagle. We have a sighting and it's the same van we saw before. Now approaching the west edge of town." Erin raised the binoculars again, being careful to stay inconspicuous. "Slowing down. I can see faces now. Looks like the van has a full load of passengers, maybe eight or ten."

"Green Eagle, have they reached your position yet?"

"Rolling slowly past us . . . *now*. Still heading east, Blue Eagle."

"Hold your position, Green Eagle. All squads, remember: do not fire until there has been an illegal act committed. We are *not* murderers, but if any of them commits a crime, shoot to kill. Once the shooting starts, it is open season on buzzards."

Gus's voice broke in. "Blue Eagle, the van is stopping between our position and the corner. Buzzards are exiting the vehicle and running toward the alley."

Will spoke up. "There's a girl back there! I think they saw her. She just spotted them . . . she took off to the east." Will stopped speaking for several seconds, then, "They caught her, and oh, no! They're going to rape her!"

"That's it." Nolan's voice was cold. "*That's it.* They are dead men. All squads except Aeries One and Two, move in now!"

"Girl is down! I repeat, girl is down!" Will sounded angry and breathless.

Hunter, Gus, and Shane burst out of their respective locations, running toward the alley. As they crossed the street, the van's tires squealed. The driver had seen them, and he took off, abandoning his pals.

In the alley, the poor young woman lay on the ground, being raped by a heavyset, bald thug when John stepped out a nearby door and shot him in the head, then turned and quickly fired at another punk. Hunter and Gus came around the corner of the building and Gus shot a mean-looking black man who was raising a gun to take John out. Gus started to fire again, but was grazed by a shot from another convict.

Shane arrived in time to take a shot at a wiry fellow who was backing away from the fight. As the punk dropped from a gut shot, Shane side-kicked another convict in the knee, crippling him for the few minutes that remained of his sorry life. Shane leaned over and rammed his knuckles into the guy's throat, crushing his windpipe, then in one fluid movement, rose and kicked another in the groin. When the man doubled over in pain, Shane grabbed his left ear, pulled him up, and drove his elbow hard, into the thin bones of the man's right temple, sending slivers of bone into the thug's brain.

Hunter dove into the middle of the fray, grabbing the girl under the arms and helping her to a spot behind a dumpster, out of immediate danger. She was in a daze, but cooperated.

"Stay here. I'll be back after we finish cleaning out the vermin," Hunter whispered.

Vince sprinted down the alley, and shot twice at a tattooed young Hispanic who simultaneously fired at Will. The Hispanic kid fell to his knees on the pavement, but tried to raise his gun once more. Vince shot him again. The kid looked stunned for a second, then slowly toppled over. Will dropped his weapon and clutched his upper arm, where blood ran freely.

Two of the convicts managed to retreat, running west down the alley toward Tanner and Erin's position. Tanner darted down the ladder, ran to the door, and stepped into their path, shouting, "Stop! Drop those guns, right now!"

One of them dropped a revolver and showed his empty hands, but the other one tried to raise his gun to shoot Tanner. Erin, looking down from the roof of the two-story building, shot the man in the upper chest. The bullet, angling steeply downward, hit several vital organs before exiting through the man's buttocks. He fell backwards, and Erin watched his eyes glaze over as blood ran from his mouth.

Almost as quickly as it began, the fight was over. The last convict knew he had no chance to escape, with both Gus and John pointing guns at him. He dropped his weapon and clasped his hands behind his head, fingers interlaced. It was obvious that he had been through that drill before. With Tanner's captive, that made two who would stand trial.

John lifted his radio wearily to his mouth. "Blue Eagle, it's over. Will is hit, gunshot to the arm. He's losing a lot of blood. Gus has a flesh wound. Notify Angie. We need transport for Will and Gus. Seven buzzards down, two captured."

Chapter 23
Late July

Nolan and Talako came tearing down the street in Erin's Expedition, screeching to a stop in a narrow parking lot between two buildings. Shane had taken off his tee shirt and had it pressed firmly against Will's arm in an effort to stop the bleeding. Ian and Shane helped Will into the seat, Shane climbing in to keep pressure on the wound. Gus climbed into the back.

Charlie, Ken, and Sarah arrived just as the big SUV sped away.

"How bad is it?" Ken asked.

John looked worried. "The bullet went through. I think he'll be okay, if the bleeding stops. He's lucky it was small caliber. Gus has a graze, and it's deep. He's a tough old bird. Stayed in the fight even after taking a hit."

"What are we going to do with the bodies?" Sarah inquired.

"Leave them where they are for now. We'll deal with that tomorrow," John sighed.

The others gathered around, the expressions on their faces a study in contrasts, from satisfied to shell-shocked. Most of them avoided looking too closely at the dead convicts. Erin's face was a blank, her eyes sad, and she was very quiet. The Gibbs twins came last, one on each side of the young rape victim, Amber. They had both known her in high school.

Ken gestured for everyone to move in close. "Amber, we would like for you to come stay at the church with us. There are several ladies there already. We'll be happy to help you in any way we can. Everyone, I think that prayer would be appropriate now, if you would join me."

Heads bowed, they prayed.

***

Wearily, the group trudged back to their vehicles, which were parked behind the church. The two captives, tied hand and foot, had been locked in the city jail. Not one of the town's three police officers was anywhere to be seen, but the keys to the cells were in a desk drawer. Heather and Hunter volunteered to stay at the jail to guard the prisoners until their trial, which would be the next morning.

***

Angie had just finished cleaning and stitching Will's arm, while Mac and Valerie cleaned and dressed Gus's graze, when the other vehicles pulled into the yard. Angie bandaged Will's wound, then gave him a pain pill that Richie had gotten out of his stock. She rinsed her hands and walked into Nolan's arms.

"Frances and Valerie prepared a light lunch for everyone. Go wash up and we'll eat a bite," she urged.

Exhaustion etched the faces of the friends seated anywhere that they could find a spot. Will was out cold, but Gus visited with Charlie while they ate.

In turn, each of the warriors quietly related his or her part in the morning's fight, except Erin, who said very little.

"I wonder where the guy in the van went," Gus scratched his head. "Did anyone see which direction he took?"

"He turned at the corner, went a block, and turned again, headed west. I bet he went back to wherever they were hiding out. Or maybe he just kept going. One can hope," Ian replied.

Plans were made to meet in town the next morning for the trial, then those who lived elsewhere left. Angie promised to check in on her patients soon, and left instructions for their care in the meantime.

Promising that one of them would be back soon with Rose, Talako and John went home through the eastern cave. Erin told them to tell Rose that she was welcome to stay overnight if she wanted, then lapsed into silence once again.

***

Rose came back with John. She sat beside her husband until he woke up. He was groggy, but smiled into her dark eyes and

147

reassured her that he would be fine. Angie gave him an oral antibiotic and another pain pill, then Rose let John lead her back home. She wanted to talk to her children and make sure that they understood that even though their daddy was hurt, he would be just fine.

Taking Erin's hand, Tanner gently led her outside to the bench on the front porch.

"Honey, I know that today was completely out of your realm of experience. Maybe it would help to talk about it, if you want. Or we can just sit here and be still. Whatever you want, I'm here."

Erin took a deep breath and let it out slowly, staring at the wooden planks beneath her feet. "I've never killed anyone before. I'm not sorry I did it, not at all, because he would have killed you. I guess it's partly shock, and partly that I wonder if something is wrong with my heart, because I don't feel the least bit guilty. Does that make me a bad person, a cold person, that I can take a life and not feel any remorse?"

"No. Absolutely not. It makes you a very brave woman. Those men were beyond evil. They would have gang raped that girl, or you, for that matter. They've killed before and tried to kill today. There was no reasoning with them. You did what needed to be done and Ernie would be proud of you."

"Do you really think so?"

"I do. He left the weapons so that you and whoever you befriended could protect yourselves and others. That's what you did today, what we all did. You stopped a bad man from killing me, and while I'm sorry that you had to do it, I'm also glad you didn't hesitate. You saved my life today, Erin. Thank you."

"You're very welcome. Funny, the only thought I had when I saw that punk take aim at you was, 'not while I'm breathing.' Those words were in my mind when I pulled the trigger. There was no way I was going to let that scumbag hoodlum hurt you, and do you know why?"

Tanner smiled. "I think I do, but tell me anyway."

Erin put a hand on each side of his face, and looking into those beautiful dark eyes, said softly, "Because I love you."

***

The next morning, Talako presided over a trial held in the abandoned feed store. Twelve adults, none of whom had been involved in the battle the previous day, were chosen to act as jurors. Some of the townspeople stood guard around the old building, although everyone hoped that the immediate dangers had passed.

Because there were no lawyers available, the witnesses just stood and told their stories. One young woman came forward and pointed at one of the defendants.

"My name is Robin Harris. That man raped me, along with a couple of his friends. They beat me and burned me with cigarettes, then laughed when I screamed." She raised the bottom of her shirt to show the burn marks on her stomach. "They let me go, but that man told me they would be back, and would bring more friends next time."

Amber testified that the two men had both been with the man who had raped her, and that they egged him on, eagerly waiting their turns. John then explained that he had witnessed the rape and saw the defendants at the scene.

The old woman who had been beaten hobbled forward, and weeping, told the jury how the two had been with the gang that broke into her house. She pointed at Weasel, and stated that he had struck her husband on the head with a tire iron. She explained that they had hit and kicked her, and beat her husband to death. She described how they stole their food, her wedding ring, and her husband's watch, then left her lying on the floor, bleeding and unable to rise.

Erin, Tanner, and Ian testified that they had seen the men actively participating in looting and vandalism, then Gus described how they had gone through the town, stealing food, liquor, and valuables, breaking windows, and destroying property.

Talako asked the defendants if they had anything to say in their own defense. Weasel refused to speak at all, and just stared sullenly at the floor.

The Hispanic man spat in Talako's direction, cursing him in Spanish before switching to English.

"You don't have the authority to try me. I know my rights. I want a lawyer! You stupid gringos can't do this to me!"

Talako explained that there were no lawyers available, and that the court was just as legal as the courts that meted out justice in the Old West. "A community has the power and the responsibility to keep its citizens safe. You have had a speedy trial, a jury, and a chance to speak out, if you have anything to say to refute the charges against you."

The man spat again, and began calling the witnesses filthy names. "I'll rape you again, stinking *puta*! You will pay for this. I will get out of prison and rape you to death!" He shouted obscenities at Robin Harris, threatening violent retribution, and screamed at the old woman that he would kill her, too.

Talako interrupted the tirade by gesturing to Tanner, who punched the man in the gut, causing him to double over and gasp for breath.

Talako stared at the man, eyes narrowed, and waited for him to look up. "You won't be escaping from prison. We won't be putting anyone in prison for a while. The prisons are closed indefinitely. What we *are* using, is the death penalty."

The jury went into the back room to deliberate, but were gone for less than ten minutes before returning with a unanimous verdict, guilty on all counts, and a recommendation for the death penalty.

The make-shift courtroom was silent after the jury foreman gave the verdict, then Talako spoke again.

"There is no reason to delay the sentencing. The accused are guilty, and they are sentenced to immediate death by firing squad. Who will volunteer to carry out this execution?"

Almost every man present, and some of the women, stepped forward. Talako selected six men and had six rifles prepared.

The two condemned men were dragged to the edge of town and tied to a chain-link fence, the Hispanic man cursing the whole time. The firing squad took up their positions in a line. Talako called out, "Ready! Aim! Fire!" and it was done.

***

A homebuilder who lived in the area and owned earthmoving equipment offered to use his front-end loader to move all the bodies, and his backhoe to dig a mass grave at the edge of a nearby field. Talako accepted, and Shane, Vince, and Ian said they would stay behind to help. The townspeople left, relieved to have the threat of the gang removed, and those who lived in the country went home as well, but Ken lingered nearby.

When the hole was large enough, the three younger men threw the bodies in. The builder began pushing dirt back into the hole, and nobody said anything, except Ken, who simply muttered, "May God have mercy on their souls."

***

Later that night, Erin and Tanner sat on their upturned buckets on the deck, holding hands and saying very little. Tanner watched the moonlight play across Erin's sweet face and knew that he had found everything he had ever wanted.

Finally, Erin turned to him and whispered, "I love you, Tanner McNeil."

He smiled and put his arm around her. "I've loved you forever, Erin. And we're going to be okay, all of us, thanks to your Uncle Ernie."

"Yes, we'll be fine. The worst is over now, and we're all alive and together."

A few minutes later, they heard someone coming up the stairs.

Ian, Vince, and Shane joined them on the deck, dirty and exhausted.

"I'm afraid we have some news," Shane frowned. "We buried those bodies, but there was a problem." He paused, letting out a long breath. "Ollie Simmons was not among the dead. Maybe that was him driving the van."

Ian added, "He's still out there somewhere. It's not over yet."

Vince's face went hard, his eyes almost blazing, but his voice would have frozen hell. "I'll find him. And when I do, I will kill him, if it's the last thing I do."

Author's Note

This is a work of fiction. Some of the locations actually exist, but the town of Kanichi Springs is a figment of my imagination. The Choctaw word "kanichi" means "anywhere."

The fact that there is a prison in the area is purely coincidental and no events depicted here are meant to reflect on the actual prison or its employees in any way whatsoever.

Yes, there really are mountains in Oklahoma. They are little mountains, but anything over 1,000 feet is considered a mountain, so these qualify.

And there really are caves in the Kiamichi Mountains, but probably none as extensive as the ones that run through Erin's mountain. There are lots of streams and natural springs in the region, as well as mountain lions, bears, eagles, deer and bobcats.

By the way, marijuana grows quite well there.

Thank you for reading Kiamichi Refuge. I hope you enjoyed it and will write a review. I would like to hear from you if you have comments or suggestions. Just visit my Facebook page (C.A. Henry) or email me at chenryauthor@yahoo.com.

Be watching for the release of *Kiamichi Storm: Book Two of the Kiamichi Survival Series*, coming soon.

Made in the USA
Lexington, KY
21 September 2017